CRUISING

SUMMER 1973: BOOK 1

DEAN CADE

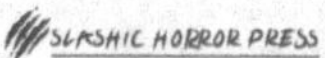

ISBN-13: 978-1-7637256-7-6

Edited and formatted by David-Jack Fletcher

Cover Design by Christy Aldridge of Grim Poppy Designs

Between 1970 and 1973, one of the country's most prolific serial killers murdered at least twenty-nine teenage boys—perhaps many more unidentified and forgotten. The killings, dubbed the Houston Mass Murders, were once considered the worst serial murders in US history.

Summer of 1973 is a fictional account of some of those lost boys.

3:07 A.M.

On the fringes of the city, close to the burn-off flares of the refineries, was Lamar Drive. Under the moonless night sky, only a few porch lights shined here and there. Muddy water ran in the bayou as faint rock music came from inside the house.

The house seemed ordinary, like all the others. Nobody had cause to suspect that whoever lurked inside was a real-life boogeyman, a predator with no remorse, and his accomplices.

A scream came from the dark house, a muffled, hoarse sound, and no one noticed. Down the street, a neighbor's dog barked before falling silent on that summer night.

An engine rumbled in obscurity as a shadowy figure opened the trunk of a dark red '68 Plymouth GTX parked in the driveway. The garage door opened, spilling out the music of The Rolling Stones's "Sympathy for the Devil". The song clicked off, leaving the sound of rustling.

Another figure joined. Hands hoisted something wrapped in plastic and dumped it into the maw of space. The weight lowered the car, creaking its suspension. The strangers kept odd hours, and the neighbors chose not to notice their comings and goings. The trunk closed but did not latch, stopped by a boot-cladded foot. A rough hand twisted it until it fit. The plastic tightened, and the rictus face of a teenage boy stared glassy-eyed through it in the dim yellow light. The trunk closed on the second attempt, and two silhouettes got into the car.

Before shutting the door, the younger driver reached into his jeans pocket, and a handcuff key fell out, tinkling on the cement. In the dark, he reached down and picked it up. The rumble grew heavier as the red GTX rolled out of the driveway and cruised down the street, leaving the sleeping neighbors unaware.

Part One

Saturday Night Cruise

ONE

THE TEENAGE BOY WATCHED the roiling clouds churn in the turbulent sky. The wind buffeted his blue coveralls. Stitched on one side was a logo of a white Pegasus, the winged horse of Greek mythology, and on the other side, a stitched patch of his name, Lane.

A storm is coming. God, I love it when it's like this. Lane's stray thought passed as he focused on the cars on the nearby road.

Shepherd Drive was a dividing line that marked the border of the Heights, a working-class neighborhood. There were sedans, coupés, muscle cars, and pickup trucks coming by steadily, with enough space between them for the road not to seem too busy.

The wind rattled another winged horse, Pegasus, on a metal sign for Mobil with a ringing echo. Lane's brown, shaggy hair whipped across his brow from the gust. He put his hands in his oil-stained pockets, feeling his house key and wallet.

A bus passed, and Lane noticed a young man in uniform. *He's probably back from a tour of Vietnam. I'm so lucky the draft is over.*

The gas-filling station bell rang as the long, metal body of a green '70 Plymouth Fury—grill covering the headlights in hard, radiator-like lines—drove in and stopped at the pump. Lane ambled over, catching the old man's eye from the garage. He averted his gaze to the car and greeted the middle-aged driver. "What's doing, man?"

"Just fill her up and wash the windows," the driver said, adjusting the collar of his brown tweed jacket.

"No problem, sir. I got it." Lane unscrewed the Plymouth's gas cap, unhooked the nozzle, and put it into the tank.

Lane turned the pump on and watched as the numbers slowly spun, clicking with each digit as the gasoline flowed. He reached into a bucket on the station island and pulled out a wet squeegee, sloshing it across the windshield.

A car honked, and Lane looked up. His casual friend, Don, who lifeguarded at the Oak Forest Pool, flashed him two fingers, the peace sign, out the passenger window of a '67 Buick GS 340. The car's body was primer gray with a low and wide red racing stipe. Lane prided himself on knowing every make and model. Another long-haired guy, whom he did not recognize, was driving and laughing with Don. Lane smiled and signed them back just in time to stop the gas from overflowing.

Lane turned off the pump, gauging the cost. "That'll be seven dollars and seventy-five cents for twenty gallons."

The man dug into his pocket and handed Lane eight bills. "Keep the change."

"Thanks." Lane flashed a smile.

The Fury drove away, ringing the service bell once again as its tires rolled over the bell's tube.

Lane eyed the clock through the dirty glass of the station office window and felt relief. *Time to go. I'm done being a tool.*

The interior of the garage was semi-dark. The only light was fading gray from outside, yet the old man still toiled on the radiator of a rough orange '69 Mustang. The old man's face was a mask of cracks and lines as he concentrated on a hose at the bottom, his arm twisting and his back heaving with exertion.

Near the office door, with a Mopar parts calendar tacked up and crooked, Lane took his time and washed the grease off his hands in the dirty sink. Xs marked off the first week of July 1973, leaving Saturday the 7th clear.

Lane smiled as he thought about the weekend. *Cruise the strip tonight*, he thought, a twinkle in his eye as he pictured Kyle's tough Challenger, *and I'm not back here until Monday. Sweet.*

Tools gleamed out of the shadows. The outside sign bent in the wind again, creating another echoing, metallic sound.

Lane walked to the orange Mustang.

Without looking up, the old man spoke, "Are you leaving already, boy?"

"It's one o'clock, Ben. Time to go." Lane tapped his foot for emphasis.

Ben sighed, rising with a screwdriver clutched in his palm, and he turned his weary head to look at Lane. "I guess it is."

"Everything all right?" Lane asked.

Ben was about to speak when the door slammed open, rattling the tools, followed by the sound of smacking gum. Jeff, the second-shift hippie, had arrived.

Lane nodded at him, then tilted his head quizzically toward Ben. "Can I go then?"

"Yeah, it can wait till Monday," the old man said, dismissing him.

Lane walked out of the garage, looked back to see Ben talking to Jeff in confidence about something, and shook his head. *Ben's nephew gets all the good shifts.*

After a quick glance around the small, dirty station office, Lane grabbed his metal lunch tin off the floor. It was the only thing at work that was his, aside from some tools. Deciding to leave it, he tucked it away on a shelf next to the desk.

Half-heartedly, he waved to the two oblivious men, who were still in the middle of some semi-serious conversation. Walking away, he put one foot after another on the road, and with a sigh, he let go of the unnecessary stress of his service job.

The sky darkened with the threat of rain, yet there was something serene about the moment—peace before chaos.

The wind buffeted Lane's unzipped coveralls, cooling out his loose boxers on the inside. The air felt soothing on his balls after his mind-numbingly repetitive shift at the Mobil Station.

Shepherd Drive felt dirty—not dirty in a seedy way, although that existed—but unkempt and forgotten. Businesses that flourished in the 1950s were rundown or closed. A sense of decay and rot permeated the air in a part of Houston left behind by the ever-expanding suburbs.

The 7-Eleven corner store, with its tasty frozen Slurpees, beckoned through the blight with its eye-catching red, green, orange, and white stripes and large number seven logo.

Paper flapped, crackling as the wind moved by. Lane's attention followed the sound. On a telephone pole, full of rusted tacks and nails, was a lone tattered flyer. Missing stood out in bold black letters across the top, and below two, side by side, pictures of scruffy teenage boys, David and Malley, and a $1,000 reward.

Lane stared at the poster for a long moment, trying to remember where he had seen them last. *Oak Forest Pool*, he thinks. *Back in the spring of '71 before I started working at Mobil.* Everyone said they'd ran away. He wished he knew where they were, because he sure could use the money.

A few cars passed, breaking Lane's train of thought as he left the old post behind. The idea of chilling out swirled in his mind as he approached the 7-Eleven. The door swung open, and an exiting teenager knocked into his shoulder, startling him.

"Hey, man, watch it." Lane knocked back.

"Sorry, I..." The teen got a knowing look in his eyes and asked, "What's up, Lane?"

"I should've known it'd be you." Lane withdrew a step. "What's going on?" *Damn, I can't go anywhere without running into Tony.*

"Not much." Tony shuffled in place, stuffing his hands deep in his pockets. "Just like anybody else stuck here."

"Right on." Lane laughed, wanting to move on. He stepped to the side, about to say 'Catch you later', when Tony stopped him.

"You got any weed, man? I'm jonesing hard for a jay."

"Sorry, man, I'm tapped." Lane fought the impulse to go inside.

"I dig." Tony fidgeted, sniffing and wiping his nose. "You gonna cruise the strip tonight?"

"Yeah, most likely it'll be me and Kyle," Lane said.

"As usual." Tony's eyes darted to someone leaving the 7-Eleven. "I don't blame you. That gearhead has a sweet ride."

"He has a 383 Magnum in that bad boy." Lane bit his lip.

"I'm jealous." Tony looked around, jittery. "Say, uh, can I ask a favor?"

Lane exhaled and looked over the loose-fitting clothes and semi-bearded face. "Tony, you know the answer."

"I just need a place to crash until my folks come around," Tony said, his voice trembling.

"They ain't coming around, not anytime soon," Lane said, having heard it before.

"I can sleep on the floor," Tony whined. It was embarrassing for him to lay down a guilt trip about crashing on a dirty floor.

"No dice." Lane shook his head. He felt bad and all, but it just wasn't happening. "The place is too small for me and Kyle as it is."

Tony looked off into the distance for a few moments, letting Lane's words disappear on the wind. "Alright," he finally whispered, "but if you change your mind, I'm getting some *goofballs* tonight."

"Sorry, I just can't do it." Lane shrugged.

"Are you sure?" Tony asked.

"Yeah, man, I'm sure." Lane stood firm.

"That's cool." A haunting look crossed Tony's eyes, then he switched, put on a smile. "See you around."

"Sure." Lane exhaled deeply as Tony ambled away.

The wind almost took the metal and glass door out of Lane's grasp. He pulled it closed with a little effort, and the store's middle-aged clerk eyed him with suspicion. Lane smiled and nodded in his general direction. Glancing at the sodas, he changed his mind and decided on the frozen machine behind the counter.

"Hey man, can I get a Slurpee swirl of Coke and cherry and some rolling papers?" Lane asked.

"What brand of papers do you want, son?" The clerk motioned behind his shoulder.

"Zig Zags, thanks," Lane said, choosing the reliable ones.

"That'll be fifteen cents," the clerk said.

Lane reached into his greasy pocket, dug into the change compartment of his wallet, and counted out a nickel and some pennies. Everything was getting expensive, they used to be twelve cents. "Here you go."

The clerk counted the change one penny at a time, then went about taking his time with the machine. Lane looked at the other brands of papers and saw Top, Bambu, Job, and Randy's—the ones that came with a wire in each one for easy rolling. His eyes moved to the cigarette packages lining the rows above. *Thirty-three cents a pack is crazy.*

The clerk pulled the lever up, leaving the cup unfilled to the top.

"Hey, pour a little more cherry on top," Lane said.

The clerk granted the request with a begrudging sigh, then slid the drink and papers across the counter with a judgmental shake of the head.

"Thanks, Pops," Lane said, snatching it up.

Lane left the store, and the strong wind tried to take the door out of his hand. Closing it, he walked on, drinking his Slurpee. Two blocks and one brain freeze later, he turned onto 27th Street and entered the Heights.

Two

Canopied by immense oaks over the narrow roadway, bungalow houses lined the sides of the street. Individual touches of color from the invisible tenants attributed faint defiance to their run-down look and the crawlspaces underneath.

Lane's thoughts drifted with the walk. *I can't believe what has happened to her since I moved out. Hell. What am I going to do?* He wished he could just talk Kyle into driving away somewhere.

A strange quiet settled in around him because of the lack of street noise. The wind bent the oak branches, drawing his attention to the creaking wood above.

"Hey, boy. Why don't you come over here? I've got a windshield that needs cleaning," a familiar voice said.

Lane's eyes refocused on the scene, and he turned his head to see Old Man Wallace sitting on his porch, as usual, having his afternoon beer.

"Sure, as long as you have another one of those." Lane pointed to the can sweating in the old man's hand.

Wallace laughed and rummaged in the chest next to his porch swing, freeing a cold one from its icy grip. "For you, always."

Lane maneuvered around the junk in the yard to greet the wizened old man. The porch swing slowed long enough for Lane to get on and pull off the tab ring from a Pearl beer can.

Wallace eyed him, chugging down half the can. "Thirsty, ain't you?"

"Damn right, especially after a hard day's work," Lane said, wiping his lips.

"You remind me of myself when I was your age," Wallace said.

"When was that?" Lane asked, taking another drink.

"I was eighteen when I enlisted in the Navy during the Second World War." Wallace's eyes seemed lost in time.

"Well, at least you were on a boat that came back," Lane said, not sure if Wallace was about to dive into a war story.

"Amen to that," Wallace said, his eyes clearing. "How's your mother?"

"She's still up at Heights Hospital." Lane sipped now, savoring the flavor.

"Tell her my prayers are with her," Wallace said.

"I will." Lane gazed blankly into the distance, seeing nothing but images of his bedridden mother in his mind. He repeated, in a hushed whisper, "I will."

"Are you and Kyle getting along in that tiny place?" Wallace asked.

"Come on, it ain't that small, but it's working out all right," Lane said.

"Good." Wallace's chest swelled. "At least you try, unlike most of the kids in this damn neighborhood."

"I like it here." Lane shrugged. "This is where my friends are."

"You're here because it's all you know." Wallace sighed. "I wish you wouldn't have dropped out."

"Don't go on telling me about school again. I made my choice," Lane said, clenching his jaw and using his feet to push forward in the swing.

"I just want better for you." Wallace chewed over his thoughts. "The Heights are decaying like some old fruit fallen from a tree."

"There are still decent people here. The Boulevard with the giant oaks and the hanging Spanish moss in front of the mansions is cool. Ain't there beauty in that?" Lane defended his home.

"There's no future here, you know that. The trees have grown wild, the mansions are in ruins. Nobody comes here. Hell, the police won't even patrol the streets at night," Wallace said, tensing up enough to dent his beer can.

The silence between them was palpable. Lane sipped his beer. A dark red '68 Plymouth GTX hardtop pulled up to a house catercorner from the porch.

Wallace slowed the swing, watched intently, and grumbled, "That goddamn Henley kid just ain't right."

Lane looked over and saw the skinny, long-haired guy—the one driving the '67 Buick GS 340 with his friend Don earlier—step out of the GTX and slink up to a bungalow house across the street.

"He sure gets around," Lane mumbled, wondering why he was in a different car earlier.

"What are you talking about, boy?" Wallace asked.

"Nothing." Lane returned his gaze. "So, what did he do to you to get you so riled up?"

Wallace took a bitter sip of his beer and squinted to get a look at whoever was waiting in the idling GTX. "Wayne is just plain bad. He's always up to something."

Lane felt eyes watching him from the darkened backseat of the car. The wind blew, sending a chill up his spine. "Hell, Wallace. You're giving me the heebie-jeebies."

"Good," the old man said, looking Lane squarely in the face. "Stay away from him and that crowd he runs with. They're trouble."

Lane smirked. "Yes, Dad."

"I *should've* been your father." Wallace sighed and said, "Only if I'd been a little younger."

"You're more of a father to me than my real old man...wherever he is." Lane gulped down the rest of the beer as thunder rumbled from far away.

Wallace's rheumy eyes left Lane for the darkening sky.

"I best get out of here before it comes down." Lane stood from the swing and crunched the aluminum Pearl can in one hand.

"All right, will you tell your mom I'm coming to see her next week?" Wallace continued to swing.

"I will. She'll like that." Lane stretched and cracked his back. "See you."

"Yeah, see you, Lane." Wallace cracked open another can and returned his gaze across the street.

Lane crossed the yard, feeling the eyes from inside the GTX on him again. He tried not to look, yet the situation bothered him as the first cold drops of rain splattered down from the heavens.

"Don't piss on me yet. I've still got a few blocks to walk," Lane said to himself.

The GTX revved behind him with a heavy rumble. Lane felt its sound shake his body as it got closer, edging up at a slow pace.

This is weird. Lane kept walking, not daring to look back. *Don't make eye contact, they'll drive on.*

The GTX slowly turned onto another street, its tires treading the concrete. The muscle car was close enough for the exhaust to warm his leg as it passed, and Lane relaxed a little when the rumble faded out.

THREE

Rain teased in droplets from the dark sky on the walk as Lane made good time with the oak branches above, giving him shelter from the coming storm.

His mind eased further with the comforting sight of the dog-eared place he called home: the Ben Hur Apartments. It was a big name for a small, two-story, red brick complex of thirty units with an open courtyard and a pool.

Kyle's super-blue '70 Dodge Challenger was out front with the hood up and the engine running. Kyle was shirtless and dirty, with oil and grease smears on his chest and jeans. He leaned over the 383 Magnum, manually checking the throttle and revving the RPM.

Lane walked up, smiling at the sight.

The Challenger was all motor—angled up from the coach with racing tires. The engine's sound, the ear-cracking roar of the beast, along with the smell of gasoline and exhaust, defined the power of the night cruise.

Lane admired the scene before him. *Damn, Kyle is lucky. I wish someone would buy me a car like that, even if they kicked me out of the house.*

Kyle let go of the throttle, and the engine calmed to a rumble. Bending upward, he brushed his sandy blond hair out of his emerald eyes, taking in the sight of Lane.

"What's going on, man?" Kyle asked with a hint of mischief.

"Hey, Kyle." Lane was enamored by his charisma. "Are you ready to party tonight?"

"You know it." Kyle brightened.

Lane smiled and nodded his head, pulling the papers out of his pocket. "Let's burn one and chill out a bit."

"That'd be cool." Kyle looked over the engine appreciatively. "I got her running like a charm."

"She's sweet, that's for sure," Lane said.

"You know it," Kyle said, revving it once more.

Lane felt a little awkward around Kyle; he always had. He shifted from foot to foot, stealing glances, but he really wanted to go inside.

The rain poured in a sudden onslaught, cold and drenching as it came down.

"Shit," Kyle said, putting the hood down and quickly rolling up the driver's side window.

Lane grabbed the toolbox and dashed for the stairs in the open courtyard, laughing. "Hurry up, you grease monkey!"

"You better run!" Kyle dashed after Lane.

The rain was heavy, making the way slippery. Up the stairs, they ran and skidded to a sliding halt in front of a door marked #19.

Kyle jabbed Lane into the upper arm and shouted, "Got you!"

"Ow!" Lane flinched.

The door slung hard toward the wall, but the stopper saved the off-white painted plaster. The apartment living room was small, with a twin bed taking up most of the space, along with a card table and two folding chairs. A ten-inch black and white Zenith with bent rabbit's ears sat atop the table amidst the clutter of empty plates, cups, and a few beer bottles.

Kyle walked ahead to the bathroom and grabbed a towel. After halfway drying off, he tossed it to Lane who wiped his face, unbuttoned his work shirt, and turned on the television. It took a moment to warm up. The picture turned from a gray landscape to a slowly clearing image of a tennis match.

Lane turned the bottom knob, and President Nixon stared at him for a moment. He clicked the knob again and tuned into a reporter, clad in horn-rimmed glasses and a tweed suit, who talked about the raid of a Texas whorehouse called the Chicken Ranch.

He turned the top knob to receive static on all fronts, then clicked the television back off and said, "Nothing is on. I hate Saturday TV."

"Play some music," Kyle said, leaning out of the bathroom with a foamy toothbrush hanging from his mouth.

"Yeah," Lane said as he got up and crossed into his sparsely furnished room. He passed his twin bed toward his dresser, where his turntable and rock and roll records took up every bit of its top space.

A random, colorful, rhombus-shaped macramé wall hanging put emphasis on the barren walls while an oak tree danced in the storm outside, its branches scratching the window pane as it moved.

Lane thumbed through album covers, including Led Zeppelin, Pink Floyd, and The Rolling Stones, before stopping on Deep Purple's *Machine Head*. He pulled the black vinyl free from its sleeve, flipped it over to the side with the track "Smoke on the Water", and placed it under the needle.

Back in the living room, Kyle lit some incense and placed it on a wooden burner. Lane plopped down on the side of the bed next to him and pulled out the damp Zig Zags, while Kyle reached under and brought up a metal rolling tray taken from a burger joint one wild night.

"Help me break this up." Kyle positioned the tray between them. "There are too many stems in this."

Lane harvested the weed. "So, what's the plan?"

Kyle sorted through the papers, settling on a dry one. "I figured we'd cruise up Shepherd, stop at the dive, pick up some chicks, and maybe head up to the drive-in or park somewhere."

"That's cool." Lane pushed the clean buds aside. "What chicks did you have in mind?"

The rain blasted the roof, and the lights flickered for a moment.

Kyle took a pinch of pot between his fingers and sprinkled it along the creased paper. "It sure is coming down."

"Quit messing around. Who?" Lane felt impatient.

Astutely, Kyle rolled it back and forth between his thumbs and the first two fingers of each hand, smoothing it out, then licking the sticky strip to twist for a finished joint. "Jenny said she'd be at the Bohemian early."

"What's the part you're not telling me?" Lane asked with trepidation.

"Oh yeah, she has a friend for you," Kyle said slyly.

"Not this again. Last time was a disaster." Lane sighed toward the ceiling. "I mean, that girl, Sally, was a wreck. Talk about homely."

"Well, I try for you, pal. I try." Kyle lit the joint, inhaling deeply.

"Nah, don't get me wrong, I'm appreciative." Lane took a hit, his mind reeling with mixed emotions for the coming night. He hoped he sounded convincing, because he wasn't ready for Kyle, or anyone, to know how he really felt.

A brief, crackly pause marked the space before the next track as the record player's needle brought out the sounds of Deep Purple's "Lazy". The drumming rain added a soothing backbeat to the song in the now-hazy room.

"No worries. Anyway, it's easier to get a girl on a double date at first than to get her alone." Kyle leaned back.

"This is cool," Lane admitted, glancing at Kyle's dirty, muscular arms. He was careful to not let his eyes linger too long.

"What?" Kyle stared at Lane through the smoke.

"I mean, this is some cool pot," Lane said, lying back to look at the ceiling.

"Yeah, it's real mellow." Kyle took another hit, passed it back, then got up to rummage through the barren kitchen. "We've got to get some food in this place one day, for Chrissakes."

Lane's eyes felt heavy, and he reached out with the burned-down joint between his fingers. "Here, take this. I don't want anymore."

Kyle took it. "Man, you're stoned. It must've been rough for—"

Lane watched Kyle through droopy eyes, not understanding what he was saying. The cherry from the joint glowed orange in the dim room as beautiful unconsciousness took him away.

Four

LANE AWOKE DISORIENTED AND sat up, rubbing his bloodshot eyes. The rain had stopped, and the sun, lower in the sky, shone twilight colors into the windows while the room was hot and humid, like a sauna.

Kyle stepped out of the bathroom, a towel barely clinging to his waist. "You fell out, Lane."

"I must've been dog-tired." Lane stretched, popping his back.

Kyle slid into a pair of jeans without underwear. "What's the news about your mom?"

Lane looked away, wishing for a different topic. Wishing the sight of Kyle sliding in and adjusting his buck-naked body into the denim wasn't so damned intriguing. "I don't know. I'm going up there on Monday to see what's up."

"It's cool if you don't want to talk about it." Kyle buttoned up a short-sleeve shirt and slicked back his hair with one hand.

"It's weird. One moment she was fine,"—Lane walked to the fridge and opened it—"and now this."

Hunting for a shoe under the bed, Kyle asked, "You okay?"

"No, not really." Lane admitted, staring inside the mostly empty icebox.

"You'll be better after a beer. I'm going to make a run. Be ready when I get back." Kyle tripped on his loose shoe and grabbed his car keys.

"You got it." Lane smiled, despite himself.

"You know it." Kyle held a magnetic grin.

The door slammed, and Kyle's loud footsteps became fainter as they descended the stairs to the gravel outside.

Lane kicked off his boots as he listened for the sound of the Challenger. *I wish I could be like him. Nothing seems to bother him, and everything's always cool. God, wouldn't that be nice?*

The smile faded as he padded across the room, then pulled off his dirty blue coveralls with the Pegasus logo and let them drop to the floor with his boxers. Naked, he walked to the mirror in the bathroom. In the reflection, he saw a pale body except for his dirty hands and face. *Not too shabby.* He flexed, impressed with the slight definition of his muscles. *Maybe I am a hunk.*

The shower ran cold at first, then began to heat to a bearable temperature. Lane stepped under the running water and felt the day melt away, swirling down the drain along with the remnants of his high. The soap worked well and took off the oil and grime with a little effort.

Lane's hand slid down, and his thoughts drifted. He tried to concentrate on a girl, Tammy, and her fine breasts, but his mind betrayed him. He imagined Kyle, shirtless and sweaty, working on his car and turning around with unbuttoned jeans, showing just a hint of blond pubic hair and the bulge below. The phantom Kyle rubbed his crotch and slowly unzipped when there was a loud knock.

Kyle slammed open the door and yelled, "Quit playing with yourself, Lane! We got to go!"

Lane awkwardly replied, "I'll be right out, man."

Kyle laughed as he backed off. "Seriously, the chicks are waiting."

"Dammit, Kyle, I said I was already," Lane said, turning and facing the shower wall.

"Save it for your girl." Kyle ducked out as a bar of soap smacked into the door, leaving an imprint.

"Get out, you freak!" Lane laughed and showered off, feeling a little blue-balled.

Dusk's golden light bathed the Heights in an otherworldly glow. Kyle hit the gas, revving the engine of his prized Challenger.

Lane locked the apartment door and ran down the stairs dressed for a hot Saturday night with slicked hair, jeans, and a T-shirt. His work boots almost scuffed the side of the door as he jumped into the car without opening it.

"Hey, watch the paint job!" Kyle warned. Satisfied that the muscle car was okay, he smiled and tossed a beer to Lane. "All set, man?"

Lane cracked open the can of Budweiser, tasting the hot beer. "Let's hit it!"

Kyle punched the car into gear, and the back tires flung up gravel and dust as they peeled out of the Ben Hur parking lot and headed up 27th Street. Through the flashing oak branches above, a crescent moon peered at them from the clear sky. Lane forgot the day, truly feeling alive at nightfall.

Kyle clicked on the radio as he turned the Challenger out onto Shepherd Drive in the cruising traffic. The DJ announced, "This is Crash in Your Dash with the Saturday Night Cruise, on Rock 101 KLOL, and this is Zeppelin."

Chords of the melancholy "Stairway to Heaven" flowed from the two speakers, transfixing Lane.

Street lights came to life with a yellow glow, illuminating the way as the sun dimmed on the strip. The scene was different at dusk. Muscle cars cruised in both directions, and all kinds of people roamed about in the colorful lights of the sparse dive bars and diners that beckoned with their enchantments.

Lane stared at Kyle, watching him drive in total control of the situation. *I wish I was normal, like him. Why can't I like girls? I don't get it. I'm just a guy who likes—*

"What're you staring at?" Kyle swigged his beer, giving Lane a curious look.

"I envy you, man," Lane admitted, snapping out of his daydream.

"Why is that?" Kyle swallowed and honked at a silver-primer '69 Mustang that veered too close.

"You get everything you want, so easy," Lane said.

"Hell, I wish it were easy." Kyle looked straight ahead. "I might get it, but I don't keep it."

Lane continued to stare as he nursed his beer. "I don't even *get* it."

"You will. Just keep your head up, man." Kyle loosened his grip on the wheel and turned the Challenger into the pothole-ridden Bohemian Pool Hall parking lot.

"I doubt I'll find it in there." Lane chugged the rest of his brew.

Kyle laughed, crumpling his empty can in his fist. "You never know where you'll find it."

"That's no lie." Lane chuckled as he also crushed his can.

They got out, swung the muscle car doors shut, and tossed their crushed cans into the oleander bushes on the side of the lot. Kyle roughly patted Lane on the shoulder as they walked to the black-painted entrance of the faded-out front of the dive.

The Bohemian was a dingy, smoke-filled pool hall sporting six tables, a bar, and a jukebox playing a country song by Cal Smith, "The Lord Knows I'm Drinking".

Five of the tables were in play with coeds and hippies, but the sixth one in the back corner had a familiar face. Don, the lifeguard, took a shot and missed.

Raising his voice over the music, Lane asked Kyle, "Who's that with Don?"

"Some cat named James. I think. We smoked down before." Kyle checked out the place. "I really don't know him well."

James, a dark-haired guy with piercing blue eyes, chalked his stick, looking out at the layout of balls on the table.

Cursing at himself, Don looked up and caught Kyle's wave, returned it. Lane nodded and stopped at the bar while Kyle headed for the corner.

"You get the first round," Kyle said over his shoulder.

"I always get the first round," Lane said, then continued to himself, "and the second and third."

The bartender, a big biker with white hair and a long unkempt white beard, sized him up. "What can I get you, son?"

Lane pulled some cash out of his back pocket. "How about four beers for me and my friends?"

The older man's eyes hardened. "Are they all old enough?"

"Of course they are. Come on, we come here all the time, Ralph," Lane said.

"Well, you take that kid out back," Ralph said, pointing at Don, "because I ain't losing my license over some punk."

"Thanks, man. Here." Lane handed out three crumpled dollar bills. "Keep the change."

Ralph pulled four cold beers out of the ice well, slid them over, and shook his head. Snatching the money, he said, "Just remember that next time I might not be in the mood for this."

"I got it," Lane said, slipping on a half-smile. He carried away the beers, two in each hand, holding on to the glass bottle necks.

Strutting across the hall, he felt the eyes of two girls and a jock on him. Lane glanced over and saw a petite redhead with wavy hair wink at him. Her brunette friend, slim and all legs, laughed at some private joke the girls shared in confidence, while the boy obviously did not share their amusement.

At the corner table, Kyle was joshing it up with Don as James shot the eight ball into the corner pocket with force.

James looked up, his ocean-blue eyes locking on Lane with a subtle nod. Something passed between them, but Lane couldn't say what. A moment, for sure, but it was so small, so hidden, that he thought he imagined it.

"Nice shot, man." Lane handed James a beer, passed another to Kyle, but hesitated with Don. "Ralph is cool, but he wants you to drink outside."

"Alright," Don said, taking the beer and holding it low by his leg. Under his breath, he mumbled, "I get no respect in this place."

"It feels so cool to be eighteen," James teased.

"Shut up. You just turned." Don smirked. "It's only been a month."

"And the world has changed." James leaned the pool cue against the wall.

"Come on, then, let's go outside before Ralph changes his mind." Kyle led the group, upset that the girls were not inside.

"Right, it's time to babysit." Lane nudged Don with his elbow.

"Be cool and lay off," Don said, irritated by the perceived judgment of the eyes watching him.

James followed last and mocked, "Don't worry, Donnie-boy, I'll watch out for you."

"Dammit, James. I mean it. Be cool," Don said, letting go of the door, hoping it would hit him.

James caught it roughly and laughed.

The outside patio was a small, chain-link fenced-in yard. A concrete slab lay from the back door about halfway out to the fence, with a few picnic tables lined on top.

The boys headed for an empty table, walking past some potheads who were smoking one under the stars.

"I can't believe those chicks aren't here," Kyle said out loud.

"Maybe they haven't made it here yet." Lane sipped his beer and looked up at the night sky.

"Jenny said she'd be here at nine, and it's almost ten now." Kyle slumped down on the bench.

"What chick is Jenny hanging with now?" Don inquired, leaning over the table.

"You already have a girl, Don, and this one is way out of your league." Kyle looked from Don to Lane's expectant face and said, "Tammy."

"Tammy is my date?" Lane tensed and tightened his lips. "You didn't tell me it was Tammy."

James watched Lane's reaction with amusement and sipped his beer.

"Well, she's Jenny's new best friend, and I knew if you knew, there'd be trouble," Kyle said diplomatically.

"Tammy is hotter than Melissa. God, I have always wanted to see her naked," Don said, beer spilling down his chin. "How did you screw up a sure thing like that?"

"I don't want to talk about it. It was just a bad night last time," Lane spat out.

"That's too bad, man," James said, full of mischief.

Lane looked at him, catching his blue eyes, and wondered what he was thinking. *Does he know? Do I look queer or something? Wait, does he?*

"Come on." James put his arm up, offering it to Lane. "Let's see what you got there."

Lane looked perplexed. "What are you talking about?"

"Arm-wrestle me! Come on, don't be a pansy." James clenched his fist, motioning for Lane to join him.

Lane raised his arms in front of him, rolling up the sleeves. "Alright, I'm down."

They clasped hands and began. The skin felt warm. James came on strong and forced Lane's arm back quickly. Lane pushed back as hard as he could and brought his arm slowly back up. They locked eyes in determination, looking to overcome each other's resistance. Muscles bulged. James was stronger, and Lane felt himself letting go to the force. His arm gave out, and James smacked it down hard to the table.

Don laughed. "Damn, you showed him."

Kyle shook his head and grunted. "I could take either of you boys."

"True, you probably could," James answered, but he kept staring, making Lane uncomfortable. His eyes were piercing. They could see him. Really *see* him. "Not bad for a gas jockey." His lips curved up on one side.

"I'll beat you next time." Lane massaged his hand.

"We'll see about that," James said, and his lip curled as he gave a knowing look.

Lane could not figure James out and could only say, "Right."

The moment broke as Don cleared his throat. "Hey, check this out," he said, revealing a primo-sized joint stashed in his pocket. "Do y'all want to try this? It's from my new connection."

"Hell yeah," Kyle said, becoming interested again. "Light it up."

Don lit the joint and inhaled a deep hit. "Here you go, man." He passed it to Kyle and exhaled smoke toward the gang.

Kyle took a quick hit and handed it to Lane. "Careful, it will creep up on you."

Tentative, Lane took it from Kyle and watched it burn, dripping resin along its side. "Where did you get this stuff from?"

"Do you know the Henley kid? He's my new—" A kick to the shin interrupted. Don yelped.

"Are you smoking it or what?" Kyle asked Lane.

"If not, just pass it to me already." James held out his hand.

"Alright already." Lane took a quick toke and passed it. Avoiding James's eyes, he said to Don, "I saw you riding around with some guy in a Buick, a GS 340, I think."

"Yeah, that was him," Don admitted. "I met him at a party the other night, and he hooked me up." Don blew smoke at Kyle, then passed the joint.

Kyle gave Don a warning look, switched gears, and asked James about his new ride. "How is that bike of yours?"

Face lighting up at the thought, James said, "It's sweet, a '70 BSA. I swear, the only thing that you can see when I ride down the road is a flash of yellow."

"Is it here?" Kyle pressed.

"Nope, I left it at home since it's a party night." James took the joint from Lane, who skipped his turn. "You're not smoking anymore, Lane?"

"I'm done for now. I already fell out once today," Lane said, feeling awkward.

"I promise I won't call you out," James said, laughing through the smoke, "even if you can't handle your high."

"Give me that." Lane snatched the joint away from James.

James mocked a shocked look for a second, then turned back to Kyle and asked, "How is loading those trucks?"

"It is what it is." Kyle looked uncomfortable.

"Are they still hiring at Trident? I need a job so I can quit being a deadhead." James put his elbows on the table.

"No. They only hire Mexican workers. It really is a crummy place. All I do is load metal rods and pipes and break my back for nothing," Kyle said, taking a gulp of beer.

Ignoring Kyle and James, Don said, "You know, another thing that's weird about Wayne Henley is that old guy, Dean, he hangs out with. That guy never said a word when I was there. He just stared at me like I was on fire or something."

"That's strange, man," Lane managed through the smoke, passing the joint back to James.

"Dean is one odd cat. He used to work at a candy store that his mom owned near the elementary school. They made pralines and stuff." James rubbed his temple and toked. "My grandmother always said to stay away from him because he ain't right."

"They score some good dope, man." Don took the joint. Sparks fell off the cherry, showering onto the wooden table. "That's all I care about. Well, that and getting laid."

"Speaking of that, we should ride." Kyle stood up and said, "I got some beer if y'all want to come along."

Don spoke slowly. "That sounds nice—mighty nice."

"You're stoned, man." James laughed and stumbled as he got up.

"He ain't the only one," Kyle said, slapping James's shoulder as he led the gang. "Come on, Lane, get up. It's going to be a long night."

Lane rose, feeling a little off-kilter. He watched James stumble again and felt okay, more so than Don, who just plain messed up. Kyle strangely seemed sober to him. *Damn, I shouldn't have smoked that last bit. I'm high, and James is messing with me. I hope the ride mellows me out.*

FIVE

ON THE FAR SIDE of the Bohemian Pool Hall's lot, the dark red GTX idled in wait. Through the thick windshield glass, two shadowed teenagers watched in cold silence as Kyle, James, Don, and Lane came out the black-painted door.

"That's him." The scruffy teenager in the passenger seat breathed out.

"There are too many of them." The long-haired blond teenage driver adjusted his glasses. "It ain't gonna be tonight."

"He's gonna be pissed." The scruffy teen watched as the gang meandered toward a super-blue Dodge Challenger.

The slow-moving traffic rumbled off Shepherd Drive. Horns honked amidst the audacious yells for attention. A lone teenage boy with a blue paisley bandana around his neck walked into the lot, looking a bit off-kilter.

The driver nudged the passenger. "He won't be so mad if he can still do his thing."

The scruffy teenager eyed the prospect. "Let's offer the guy a ride."

"Okay." The driver put the GTX in gear. The tires shifted through the gravel as the muscle car rode beside the teen.

"Hey, do you want to hang out and party?" A disarming voice offered through the rolled-down passenger window.

"Um, I don't know." The teen hesitated, checking his pockets. "I need to meet my friends. They're cruising the strip."

The driver revved the engine with a tap of his foot.

"We can drop you off after." The scruffy teenager bobbed his head and reached down, revealing a bag of pills. "I got some goofballs."

The teen bit his lip. "I guess it'd be cool."

"Come on." The door opened, whining on its hinge. "Get in."

"Alright, as long as you promise." The teen scratched his chin as he climbed into the backseat.

"We're cool. You can trust us," the driver mumbled, shifting the clutch.

The door slammed shut, and the GTX idled off toward the strip.

The scruffy teenager in the passenger seat looked back at Lane and whispered, "There's always the next time."

Six

In the dusty parking lot, the foursome hovered around the trunk of the Challenger. Lane noticed the signs that Kyle had a buzz, and he also noticed James's smile as Kyle fumbled with the keys.

Kyle passed out the beers. In the soft light from the trunk, they all popped the tab rings, tasting the foamy brew before it spewed over. Four more cans flew into the oleander bushes. Kyle shut the trunk—killing the light—and walked around rough and tough, sliding into the driver's seat. Lane bumped into James as they both tried to get to the passenger's side, but Don got there first.

"I got shotgun." Don grinned from ear to ear.

"What the hell? I hate sitting in the back." Lane felt forlorn about losing his spot.

"Come on, man. You always get to cruise in the front seat," Don said, holding up the seat while drumming his fingers on its side.

"Get in the back and let's go," Kyle said impatiently.

"Alright, I'm getting in." Lane squeezed in the back, settling in behind Kyle.

Don let go of the passenger seat. It slammed back into position on the other side, leaving little space behind.

James scrunched his body, squeezed in, and adjusted his feet. "Guess it's you and me now."

There was something in the way he said it. Underneath the words. A hint of something secret passing from James to him.

"Sure," Lane said, looking at James and wondering what was up with the guy.

Kyle cranked the ignition, and the radio turned on louder than the roar of the engine. The Rolling Stones's "Angie" flowed in a melancholy way out of the speakers.

Tires peeled out on the loose gravel in the parking lot as the Challenger spun off onto Shepherd Drive, barely missing an oncoming car that blasted its horn.

Don's grin spread wider as Kyle shifted gears and punched the gas, speeding up to sixty, then easing back down into the Saturday night cruise. It was a wild atmosphere on the street, with cars jammed on each side of the road and a cacophony of teenage screams, honking horns, and big block engines.

Kyle spilled some of his beer on his lap and cursed, swerving the car again. James's legs slammed into Lane's, and he laughed, trying not to spill his own beer. Lane sipped the foam off the top of his can and made sure he kept it held up straight.

Kyle settled into cruising speed. Turning the music down a bit, he looked over at bright-faced Don and asked, "How did you end up with Melissa? That girl deserves better than a lifeguard."

"She knows a good thing when she sees it." Don puffed himself up with pride.

"She should get her eyes checked." Lane joked from the backseat.

"Shut it, Lane." Don glared back briefly.

Kyle honked at some wild girls in a cherry-red '67 Pontiac Grand Prix convertible, going the opposite way. "Where is she, anyway?"

"She has to work late at Long John's. Some kid named Jamie didn't show up, so she has to stay until closing time." Don looked for cops—none were in sight—and drank his beer. "It's kind of weird that Jamie just took off and left his El Camino there."

"Why would he leave his ride?" Lane cradled his beer can in his hands.

"Actually, it was his parents' old car. They just let him use it," Don said.

"Maybe he wanted a new start. You know, just leave it all behind and hitch to California." James followed his thoughts. "Leave all this behind and never look back."

"I wish I could hit the road." Kyle joined in with a distant look in his eyes.

Lane stretched and felt the warmth of James's leg against his. "One day, I'll get out of here."

"You and me both." James smiled slyly.

Kyle tuned into the moment. "Look, it's Troy and Angie over at the burger joint, and Jenny is there, too. Hang on, I'm turning in."

The Challenger veered sharply to the right and rumbled into the small, packed lot. Kyle managed the tight turn to pull into a spot next to the dumpster, among the seven other cars crammed for lack of space.

The burger joint was a small, green, boxy building with a yellow roof and nowhere to sit inside. A green sign with yellow puffy letters held the moniker Someburgers. The sides of the building had similar signage with Hamburgers, French Fries, Onion Rings, Hot Dogs, and Fish in a yellow, fat letter font.

The gang got out of the car. Kyle headed straight over to Jenny in a puppy-dog-like manner. Don wandered in a stoned daze to the line at the order window of the Someburgers' box. Neither one of them looked back.

Lane stayed by the car, watching the crowd with James at his side.

James nudged Lane. "It sure is a circus here, man."

"You can say that again," Lane said, shifting from foot to foot uncomfortably.

"Aren't you going to go see Tammy?" James inquired with a sly look, his words disguising an undercurrent of something he didn't know how to identify. But it was there.

"In a minute." Lane sighed. "She's mad at me."

"What did you do? Did you get freaky or something?" James ribbed.

"No! It's nothing like that, I swear. She just—" Lane broke off and changed the topic. "You want to get some fries and Coke or something?"

"It's cool if you'd rather hang with me than that hot chick over there. I understand." James laughed, stepping closer to Lane.

"Shut up." Lane chuckled at the ridiculousness of the situation, inhaling James's natural scent. He pushed James back a little; a gentle, careless motion. "It's not like that. I just need a minute to chill."

"If you say so." James shrugged. "Buy me a soda, then. I got cottonmouth."

"Come on, James," Lane said, leading them to the line. He caught a hurry-up look from Kyle across the way and ignored it.

Glassy-eyed Don bumped into them. Spilling some of his soda, he said, "I got the munchies baaaad."

"That's because you're always stoned." James punched Don in the arm.

"Not always," Don said, stumbling as he walked on.

"That cat is a mess," Lane said out loud.

"He's cool," James said, referring to the stoner predicament as the line moved forward. "Anyway, nobody scores ace weed like he does, especially around here."

"I can't argue with you there," Lane said, feeling high.

A teenage girl, clad in a green uniform of shirt and shorts, a visor holding back the front of her long ponytail, slid open the glass window. "What can I get you two?"

"I want some fries and a couple of Cokes." Lane reached into his back pocket for his wallet. "Please," he added.

The girl chewed her gum. Eyeing James, she said, "Anything else?" The 'please' had maybe come too late, and she was stuck on Lane's demanding tone. I want, I want.

James bit his lower lip and asked, "How about your number?"

"My boyfriend is on varsity. Sorry." She turned back to Lane, held out a hand palm-up. "That'll be a dollar." She raised her eyebrows as if to add, "Now, loser."

Lane dug out a bill and passed it to her, smiling as the window slammed shut.

"I think she likes me," James said.

"Right," Lane replied. He felt unsure as he stared at James, wondering about the depths and complexities of this guy, then broke eye contact and looked away at the table with Kyle and his friends.

Kyle caught Lane's eye and yelled, "Hurry up already!"

Lane masked a smile and yelled back, "All right!"

James looked at the group, then back to Lane, his smile fading a bit. "Hey, we should hang out sometime. I mean, I dig you. You're a cool guy and all."

I dig you. Lane brightened. "How about tomorrow? We're loading up and going to the beach."

"That'd be chill!" James's smile returned in force.

The girl reappeared with a fry basket and two sodas in hand.

James touched her hand and asked, "Can I use your pen?"

"I said I had a boyfriend." Recoiling as she shook her head, wagging her ponytail back and forth.

"It's not for that," James said with a chuckle.

She seemed oddly disappointed as she freed a pen from behind her ear and passed it out.

Kyle yelled again, "Come on, Lane! You are taking all night!"

"Hold your horses! I said I was coming!" Lane felt frustrated.

James grabbed a napkin, wrote his seven-digit telephone number, and scrawled James next to it. "Here you go. Call me after 10. I live with my parents, so you know how it is."

"Cool," Lane said. He looked at the paper and tucked it into his wallet. "I'll call you in the morning."

"See you tomorrow, Lane." James took his Coke and walked to a different table where Don was feasting on his burger with some other teenagers.

Lane watched James go, feeling like he was missing something. He could not quite shake the sudden loss of him, so he cracked his back, picked up the basket and drink, and walked to the other table.

The vision that came into focus was Kyle whispering in Jenny's ear, followed by laughter about a secret joke. Sitting next to her was Tammy, sipping her soda.

Nonchalant, she looked up, matching Lane's gaze with an even stare.

Lane admired her fiery red hair and broke the awkward silence. "You look good, Tammy."

She stared at him, daring him to say anything else, then said, "I know," and sipped her drink again.

Kyle kissed Jenny's neck, and she giggled, half-heartedly pushing him away before drawing him back in for more.

"Would you like some fries?" Lane set the basket on the table, then delicately set himself down on the bench next to her.

Without a word, Tammy took a couple of fries and put them in her mouth. She ignored Lane, staring at the scene like it was a sporting event of considerable interest.

"Nice night," Lane said, gulping.

Two drunken guys chasing each other around the parking lot, whooping and hollering aloud, interrupted the moment. Tammy stared into the distance, indifferent.

Lane looked across the way. James and Don were sitting with some girls at a table, and Tony sat down next to them. *You've got to be kidding me. Tony is hanging out with them?*

"Hey, Lane. How are you doing?" Jenny got out of Kyle's hold, playfully slapping his roving hand.

"Good, I guess." Lane scratched the side of his head.

Seeing James's profile, Lane felt a tingling sensation in his stomach. *Damn, I would rather hang out with him.*

"Kyle talks about you a lot," Lane said.

"He does, does he?" Jenny bit her lower lip and blushed a little, flashing her tinted eyelashes at Kyle.

"You know I do, babe. I think about you every day." Kyle felt around her leg.

"Oh yeah? What do you think about?" Jenny twirled a loose curl of her hair.

"I think about how you smell like honeysuckle in the morning. I think about kissing you..." Kyle trailed off into dirty whispers in her ear.

Tammy rolled her eyes, gave a low "Ugh," and continued to pretend Lane did not exist. In return, he sucked up the last of his soda with an agitated, slurping noise that annoyed her even more.

Looking back across the way, Lane watched as everyone at the table grabbed a blue pill, popped it into their mouths, and chased it down with a straw drink of soda. His anger flashed at the injustice. *Why can't I be doing that?*

Jenny broke away from Kyle's bite, and a hickey was forming on her soft, pale skin. "Lane, how's your mom doing?"

Lane set his Styrofoam cup down a little too hard, rattling some ice out onto the tabletop. His glance darted from Tammy, whose eyes softened just the slightest, and back to Jenny's smile. "She's doing as best as she can with being in the hospital and all," Lane muttered.

"My prayers are with her. She always was such a sweet lady," Jenny said softly.

Was? "Well, she still is. She's going to be all right," Lane replied harshly.

Flashing a warning look, Kyle butted in. "Jenny, baby, do you want to go to the beach with us tomorrow? It's supposed to be sunny."

"I would love to." Jenny turned to Tammy. "Will you go? I hate to be alone with these crazy boys." She rolled her eyes, playful and pleading to her friend.

Eyes flaring with rage, Tammy said, "I'm sure I have to go to church or something, it being Sunday and all."

Jenny grabbed Tammy's arm and pulled her aside, whispering something. Then to Kyle and Lane: "We'll be right back, going to freshen up real quick and have some girl talk."

Furious at the indiscretion, Tammy went along. Jenny smiled brightly, belying her own mood, and dragged Tammy on toward the back of the green building.

As soon as the girls left his sight, Kyle's smiled faded and he turned on Lane. "What the hell are you doing? I need you onboard tonight."

"I'm sorry, man. Tammy has it out for me." Lane forced himself to look up.

"Well, fix it. Tell her she looks pretty, and what happened last time was a fluke," Kyle said.

"I was drunk." Lane shook his head. "Dammit, I don't want to talk about this."

Kyle put his hand on Lane's shoulder and said, "Listen, just be a trooper and figure it out."

"Okay, I'll be cool with her." Lane sighed. The girls came out of the restroom, and he narrowed his gaze on Tammy. He watched them slow-walk back together, locking eyes, while she talked in an exaggerated way with Jenny.

"Look, Jenny is hot for me, if you know what I mean," Kyle said, his warm breath touching Lane's cheek.

Lane continued, "I'll take Tammy off by herself and smooth things over at the drive-in."

"I swear to God, you have me worried sometimes." Kyle smiled, catching Jenny's face as she ended her talk with Tammy.

"But Kyle, I'm only doing it for you, pal," Lane said. He showed his teeth, matching the feeble smile that Tammy threw at him.

Kyle gave Lane a sideways look and stood up, embracing Jenny. "Let's get out of here. The new *Apes* movie is at the drive-in. We can catch the second show if we go now."

"Those movies give me the creeps." Jenny snuggled closer to Kyle.

"Come on, Jenny, it is a bunch of rubber masks and barely hidden racial slurs, and they call it entertainment," Tammy said with disgust.

Jenny elbowed her. "You used to like them, remember?"

"I grew up since then." Tammy calmed down and said, "But I'll see it for you."

"Good, it's settled. Take us to your chariot, baby," Jenny cooed to Kyle.

"This way, ladies," Kyle said as he led the way. The girls were close to him, caught in the invisible tow of his take-charge attitude.

Trailing behind, Lane rose from the table and adjusted the front of his pants, brushing salt away. The trio had not even registered his absence yet. He took a moment to look at his lost friends for the night and envied their good time. James noticed him and smiled, then nodded. Lane nodded and smiled back as he trotted to the Challenger, just in time to slide into the silence of the backseat with

Tammy. He remembered how warm James's leg had felt earlier, how his own skin had tingled, how his heart had beat just a little faster.

Kyle revved up the 383 to impress the girls, and it worked, even melting a little of Tammy's ice in the air of excitement. She looked out the window, turning her head away, but Lane saw her expression, the hint of a fire in the eyes. The car peeled out onto the strip in a blue streak, and Lane caught James still watching him as they took off into the night. The image was fleeting, but it stuck with him.

The music was a blessing, Alice Cooper's "No More Mr. Nice Guy" drowning out any chance of conversation. The tough lyrics calmed Lane as they cruised by the familiar joints and dives of the Heights.

Memories flooded back as the drugstore with its checkered diner counter went by, reminding him of all the times he spent eating out with his mother. Those were simpler times, when there seemed to be no worries and no pressure. In his mind's eye, he imagined her drinking tea with a face framed with long brown hair and dotted with freckles. The memory reinforced that she was an always-loving mother, no matter what.

No matter what... Lane swallowed hard, hoping that when the time came, it would be true.

The old laundromat with its mostly broken machines passed by the car and reminded him of waiting for his mother to finish the clothes after elementary school while reading comic books like *The Amazing Spider-Man* and *The Fantastic Four*.

"Hey, Lane!" Kyle yelled over the music.

Lost in the warm nostalgia of Peter Parker and Johnny Storm, Lane did not hear him.

"Hey, Lane, take this." Kyle passed back his beer from earlier. "Jenny hates when I drive with it."

Lane snapped out of his reverie, took the warm beer, and sipped it with an uncertain face. Jenny laughed appreciatively and rocked her head back and forth to the music, while Tammy was in her own thoughts, looking out the window on her side, her face hidden by her hair.

The music stayed loud, even after Kyle's minute adjustment of the volume. Unheard by the others, Lane sighed as he looked out at the cruising cars. The road shifted in a curve, and a white '68 Pontiac LeMans with a green hardtop honked its horn, barely missing a merging dark red car. Leaning closer, Lane saw the red hood of the muscle car move in.

Is that the same Plymouth GTX from the Henley house? Remembering Old Man Wallace's warning to stay away from the crowd, Lane strained to see who was inside. The bespectacled, long-haired driver wasn't familiar, and the passenger's head had turned away. In the backseat, he saw an uncertain teenage boy smoking a joint, and they locked eyes for a moment. The boy tugged at his blue paisley bandana, and Lane felt a chill until a gap opened up in the traffic, and the GTX sped off, breaking the spell.

Lane didn't like the vibe. Something about it made him uncomfortable. The scenery changed, becoming more rural as they headed to the countryside, and he let the bad vibe drift away.

SEVEN

THE DRIVE-IN WAS A one-screen affair not far out of the city limits, though it felt like another place. A marquee marked the entrance with the double feature of *Conquest* and *Battle for the Planet of the Apes*.

Cedar shake shingles made up the back side of the screen, with SHEPHERD boldly painted on top and *Drive-In Theater* scrawled below. A framed, hand-painted mural of a palm tree swaying in the beach breeze with the sun setting over the water and three stars above added a surreal touch.

The beach scene is cool, but it makes no sense out here. Lane shifted in his seat, envying Jenny and her blind happiness. He looked at Tammy, who had turned away, like there was something fascinating in the corrugated tin walls of the drive leading inside. *I hope the movie is good, at least.*

Its 383 Magnum engine idled hard as the Challenger pulled up to the ticket booth.

A middle-aged woman with her hair up in a bun impatiently looked in and said, "It's two dollars a carload."

Kyle dug in his pants for some cash and said, "Here you go."

The woman nodded, tucked the money into her register, and picked up a book whose cover had an odd rabbit staring across a field.

Kyle punched in the knob, darkening the headlights as he drove along the high side fence to turn around toward the screen. The Challenger drove past rows and rows of lined-up cars, while Clint Eastwood leered out from the screen, daring anyone to mock him. There were lots of muscle cars with dates or rambunctious teenagers, and even a few families in station wagons braved the venue on a Saturday night.

A spot on the third row was open, and Kyle eased in. Jenny repositioned herself to see the backseat, giving Tammy a pleading look. Enraptured with the projection, Lane tried not to notice.

On the drive-in screen, a raven-haired western beauty was saying something about the gunslinger being a man who makes people afraid. The tinny noise that came out of the small speakers on metal poles—some hooked into nearby car windows—did not do the picture justice.

Lane strained to hear and caught the gist of Clint's response: "It's what people know about themselves on the inside that makes 'em afraid."

The trailer cut to clips of gunfights in a sepia-toned town and the title, *High Plains Drifter*, followed by Coming Soon.

"That's going to be good. I love westerns." Kyle smiled as he opened the door, flooding the car with a yellow light. "Who wants a beer?"

"I do," Jenny said, batting her eyelashes playfully.

"Get me one too," Tammy said. Her eyes focused on the screen as the image changed to racing cars and teenagers partying in the wild 1960s.

"Hey, let me out, man," Lane said, pushing at the seat.

"Hold your horses and let me get the latch." Kyle reached down and pulled the lever.

"Thanks. I just need to stretch, that's all." Lane met Kyle's questionable look with one of his own.

Inside the car, the girls talked to each other in hushed tones. Kyle strummed his fingers on the seat, and as soon as Lane squeezed out of the way, he pushed it back into place.

"That's *American Graffiti*, the one about the cars," Lane said, thumbing at the screen.

Kyle pulled Lane by the arm to the back of the car and opened the trunk. "I don't care about the movie, and you will *not mess up my date.*" It wasn't rage in his eyes so much as pleading desperation.

"But the show is about to start," Lane said weakly, knowing it was useless.

"Lane, take Tammy to the concession stand. Tell her something—tell her anything. I don't care. Just give me some time with Jenny." Kyle softened his look. "Do it for me."

Lane looked into Kyle's emerald eyes and caved. "Alright, I'll do it."

"Good." Kyle sighed and passed Lane a warm beer, grabbing three more in a bundle. "Wait here a moment."

"Okay. Kyle..." Lane fumbled his words.

"What?" Kyle asked.

"Uh, never mind. It's cool." Lane managed a grin.

"Hey, the girl is hot. All you have to do is warm her up." Kyle nudged Lane with his usual good-natured routine.

"Right on." Lane swigged his beer and watched Kyle work his magic on the girls through the back window.

Headlights flashed, blinding Lane for a second. The glare faded, and he realized the trunk was up, and the '68 Mustang behind him could not see the screen. He gave a meek wave and quietly shut it with a dull clunk.

Hearing the metal whine of the passenger door and the crunch of soft shoes on gravel, Lane looked up from the ground to see Tammy at his side.

"I guess I can't hate you forever," she said.

"You don't have to do this." Lane looked her over.

"What else am I going to do when those lovebirds are my ride?" Tammy asked, grimacing.

"I'm sorry, Tammy. I..." Lane trailed off in thought.

"Not here." Tammy grabbed Lane's hand and led him down the row, away from the car.

Lane followed, looking to the side and up at the goofy cartoon images of talking hot dogs, popcorn, and drinks. His nerves rose and fell as the jingle music filled his head. *"Let's go out to the lobby—Let's go out to the lobby—Let's go out to the lobby to get ourselves a treat."*

Out of the row, they turned toward the back, where the concession stand beckoned with its white brick walls.

Tammy squeezed Lane's hand, then pulled away, self-conscious.

Staring at her, Lane wished he could make her happy. "We should finish these beers and get a snack."

"You mean chug this." Tammy brightened and laughed.

"If you want to." Lane felt the tension melt as he raised his can.

Tammy raised hers. She turned it back and forth, judging its contents. "Here's to those dirty apes."

Lane laughed at her wit, clunking his can into hers. "Yes, to those damn dirty apes."

Together, they guzzled the contents as fast as they could. Tammy delicately wiped a trickle of beer from her chin. Lane was a mess.

Some beer spilt down the front of his shirt, and he spat foam onto the ground.

The sound of tinny drums and horns coming out of the drive-in speakers grabbed his attention. On the drive-in screen, spotlights roved about the 20th Century Fox logo, then the picture faded to black. The Lawgiver, a humanoid orangutan, appeared, telling the story of the apes from some future point.

Lane tried to ignore it, but he really wanted to watch the film.

Tammy mocked him. "You're a mess, Lane."

"I try. What can I say?" Lane turned away from the screen, wiping at his shirt, flecks of foam spattering to the dirt.

"Look, Lane, I know you were drunk the last time we went out, but you crossed the line," Tammy said.

"I know. I was stupid, and I shouldn't have done that," Lane admitted, sheepish, still wiping at his shirt. A clump of beer foam was soaking into his fingers and he dragged his hand across the back of his jeans.

Tammy slapped Lane in the face, shocking him. "I should've done that then."

Lane opened his mouth, then closed it. Rubbing the side of his jaw, he felt the sting and said, "I deserved that."

"Yes, you did." Tammy smiled, enjoying the awkwardness of the moment. "Now buy me some popcorn."

Lane shook his head. "Sure. Is there anything else I can get you while I'm at it?"

"We'll see when we get inside." Tammy walked ahead, leading the way again.

Jesus, is this how it is? I really don't want to understand women. I just don't get them. Lane followed her like she was a feral cat.

The small concession stand's double doors opened to an empty food line with a grill in the back and a soda fountain. Film posters, in glass cases, prominently displayed the current *Apes* films and a few upcoming features. *American Graffiti, Cleopatra Jones,* and *Enter the Dragon* all hung in lurid, comic-drawn detail.

Lane watched Tammy look over the menu and lick her lips. A bored, gruff worker came out from behind the grill and grabbed a pencil and an order pad off the greasy counter. Lane's eyes roamed the concession stand, finding a yellow poster for the movie he was reluctantly missing and a pinball machine in the corner.

"What can I get you, darlin'?" the worker asked, seeming more interested after his eyes had finished taking in Tammy's figure.

"Some popcorn, a soda, and a hot dog," Tammy said, winking at Lane. "Plus, whatever he's having."

The worker repositioned the hat on his head, hiding the greasy curls. Almost a drawl, he asked, "What do you want?"

"A Coke and a hot dog." Lane squinted at Tammy.

"Will that be all?" The worker rubbed the slight stubble on his chin and peeked at Tammy's legs.

"Yeah, I think that'll do it." Lane handed a couple of bills over the counter and guided Tammy to the pinball machine. "Let's play some pinball, you know; give them some time alone."

Tammy moved her weight from one leg to the other. "Jenny wanted me here to look after her."

"Well, it's not like he's going to go all the way in the car," Lane said.

"True, but we'll go back in thirty minutes. A girl has got to keep her promises and the reputation of her friend intact," Tammy said.

"What if Kyle ain't that bad of a guy?" Lane pulled some loose change out of his pocket and let it slide out to rattle on the glass top.

"Sure he is." Tammy glared. "All of you are."

Lane lowered his head. "I said I was sorry for Chrissakes."

Tammy leaned on the machine, covering the Gottlieb logo near the left flipper, and said, "I forgive you this time, but if you do it again, I will sic my brother on you. Do you hear me?"

Lane looked up in shame. "I hear you, Tammy." He put a quarter into the slot and got four game credits.

The space-themed machine came to life with its player scores zeroed out. A painted cartoon of a strapping astronaut looked concerned at the stars, while a female beauty at his side showed terror in her drawn eyes.

Lights flickered and raced, then the ball bounced out into the shooting slot. Lane pulled back the plunger and popped the ball into the bumpers, gaining points as it knocked them. Lane slammed the flippers and slapped the side of the machine, hoping to get the ball just where he wanted it. He felt tough, releasing some aggression from the tense evening.

Tammy sided up closer, wriggling her rear in a teasing way for whoever may be watching. "It's cool to see you're good at something."

Slamming the flipper hard again, Lane barely caught the edge of the quicksilver ball to chunk it back up. "I have my moments."

"What were you trying to prove, being such an animal that night?" Tammy asked.

Lane missed the silver ball, forfeiting his turn. "I..." He didn't know how to be honest in these moments. He just couldn't, and shrugged instead. "I don't know." Lane stepped away from the pinball machine while the game reset for the next player. "I was just trying too hard."

Tammy looked at Lane sideways and asked, "You haven't been with a girl, have you?"

Lane smiled, but it was laced with nerves. "Sure, I have. I just—"

The concession bell rang for their food order.

"No, you've not," Tammy whispered, seeing straight through his act.

Lane tilted his head, speechless at the moment.

"Here you go!" The worker slid a tray to the edge of the counter, watching with an intense stare at Tammy's wiggling.

Lane walked over, grabbing the food tray, some ketchup, and napkins, and the worker disappeared back behind the grill.

Back at Tammy's side, he offered her a weak smile and a Coke.

"It's okay; it can be our secret." Tammy took the proffered drink, putting the straw between her lips and slurping. "It's your turn."

Lane looked at Tammy, not liking the moment. He returned to pinball, and with an audible sigh, he played his next round. Concentrating on the game, he said, "I'm eighteen, and it just hasn't happened yet. I'm sorry for pawing at you that night, but I wanted to be like everyone else."

Tammy nodded with a knowing stare. "You're different, Lane, and that's okay."

"How am I different?" Lane asked.

The space pinball machine lit up with another thousand points.

"When guys want me, I sometimes have to fight them off." Tammy sized Lane up. "You were drunk and desperate that night, but you weren't interested in me."

"I'm not a bad guy, Tammy, and I promise it won't happen again." Lane didn't feel like playing anymore and missed a shot on purpose.

"No, I guess you're not." Tammy pulled back the plunger and watched the silver ball streak around the board, popping down plastic cards with alien ships on them.

"I hope that's true," Lane muttered.

"You're something else, that's for sure." The ball zoomed down the center, out of reach of the flippers. "Let's eat. I couldn't beat your score if I played all night."

"Well, you've beaten me plenty and I have the bruises to prove it." Lane laughed and bobbed as Tammy took a mock swing at him. "How about we take it outside and watch the movie?"

"Okay." Tammy felt at ease for the first time. "You know, you can be all right when you try, Lane."

He fought the impulse to tell her the truth, but he knew more than anything else that it would destroy him if he did. Instead, he said, "I like you too," and held open the door.

Tammy passed through it. "As friends." She looked at him as she spoke and he realized she knew it was more than him being a virgin. She knew he was *different*. Maybe his unspoken secret was safe with her as long as they didn't acknowledge it.

The concession doors shut, and the tinny sound of apes in battle filled the night air. Lane sat next to Tammy at a wooden table. They had a clear view of the projected film over the sea of cars.

Lane mumbled, "Friends," as he looked up at the strange western take of the cinematic war, with gorillas on horseback shooting rifles at humanoid chimpanzees. *If the guys hear that she wants to be friends, I'll never live it down.*

He arranged the meal in front of them and asked, "Tammy, do you think... Am I handsome?" His hand traced his jawline as he spoke.

Tammy took a bite of her hot dog and looked at Lane with a peculiar face. "Yeah, you're handsome enough."

"What is it about me that you don't like?" Lane asked.

"I don't know." Tammy chewed a mouthful and swallowed. "You're just not my type."

"I see." Lane watched the battle on screen, not really registering it at all, and asked, "Who is your type?"

"Somebody hot, like Kyle," Tammy said.

"You think Kyle is hot?" Lane set down his half-eaten hot dog.

"Yeah, he's dangerous, and that makes him sexy." Tammy lost the dreamy look in her eyes. "I shouldn't be talking to you about this."

Lane resumed eating, and in between bites, he said, "Well, I can be like him if I want."

"You're different. Some guys have it, and some—" Tammy let the rest of the sentence die on her lips.

"And some don't. I guess I should take that to heart." Lane looked away, sullen, and saw a couple pass by, arm in arm, the sight adding to his jealousy.

"You'll make somebody happy, just not me." Tammy cupped Lane's hand in her cool one.

"Hell, I wish I could be the bad boy for a change and get the girl," Lane said, feeling relieved on another level. *I'm just glad I don't have to tonight.*

"Just be yourself and don't pretend," Tammy said, hinting at the unspoken secret.

"Okay, I will." Lane leaned over the wooden table and kissed Tammy on the lips. She didn't recoil, didn't move away. It was a soft, platonic kiss, one imbued with understanding that they would never go all the way.

"Well, it looks like we weren't the only ones having some fun." Kyle shattered the scene by clapping Lane on the shoulder.

Tammy smiled and took in the sight of Kyle like a cool drink of water. "No, it's not what you think."

"Tammy, you're such a trooper. I'm so glad you're here." Jenny was beaming with a slight blush, making her cheeks rosy.

Awkward as usual, Lane stuffed a handful of popcorn into his mouth, watching his friends as he chewed.

"Lane has been a perfect gentleman for your information." Tammy stood and grabbed Jenny's hand. "Come on. We need some private girl talk."

"Oh, Tammy, Kyle's been nice," Jenny said, knowing that Tammy knew her all too well.

"Come on." Tammy pulled Jenny along and playfully pushed Kyle out of the way. "Why don't you zip your zipper up, Romeo?"

"Oh, shit!" Kyle looked down and quickly zipped up.

The girls walked away, Tammy smirking as Jenny's face turned crimson.

Lane chewed up the popcorn and laughed.

Kyle double-checked his pants and looked at Lane. "And don't you start with me."

"You're such a stud." Lane chuckled. "Did you?" Lane wondered how far Kyle had gone.

Kyle sat close and said in a lower voice, "Jenny, she let me take her top off. Oh man, she has some nice tits with some perky, pink nipples."

Feeling Kyle's breath on his ear, hearing the excitement in his voice, Lane pressed him on. "So then, what'd you do?"

"I swear she's wearing painted-on pants. I tried unbuttoning them, and I couldn't do it. God, it was driving me crazy," Kyle said in a low voice.

"Did you pull it out?" Lane asked.

"Nah. She started rubbing me and—" Kyle's eyes widened. "Shhh, here they come."

Lane felt the loss as Kyle scooted away, raiding the popcorn bag.

"Did you miss us?" Tammy gave Kyle the evil eye.

"Uh huh," Kyle managed through a mouthful of popcorn.

Jenny ran her hand through Kyle's hair and said, "Let's light one up and finish the movie."

Lane looked surprised. "That's the best idea I've heard all night."

"I have a special one in the car for this occasion." Kyle chewed with a big grin.

"Don't forget, Jenny. We have to be at my house before it gets too late," Tammy said.

"We have time for one, though." Jenny rubbed her hand along Kyle's biceps. "Don't be a fuddy-duddy."

Tammy laughed despite her mixed feelings and said, "One o'clock, that is as late as it gets, and you better have some good pot."

The foursome walked straight past a red Plymouth GTX on their way back to the Challenger. Lane did a double take, then realized it was not the same car—no hardtop, a different shade of red—not the one with the teenage boy who he had locked eyes with. A strong arm nudged him from staring at the GTX.

Seeing Kyle's smirk, Lane noticed the couple making out in the front seat and shrugged. Embarrassed, he plopped into the back of the Challenger first, holding the seat for Tammy, who took her time. Next, Jenny jumped in the passenger seat, laughing.

The trunk closed with a resounding thud. Kyle passed out beers in the car. Closing his door, he reached up to the visor and pulled out a joint. Repositioning the speaker on the window, he lit it up, taking a hit and filling the car with smoke.

Jenny took the joint with a delicate touch and puffed on it. "If my mother only knew."

Tammy responded, "Then you'd be living at my house." She smoked the grass like a connoisseur. "This movie is dumb."

Lane mocked a hurt look. "I like these movies."

"You would." Tammy passed it to him.

Kyle positioned himself so he could see the backseat in the rearview mirror and watch the movie with barely a movement of his head. "Come on now, the apes are cool."

Jenny giggled and said, "If you say so."

"No, they really are. Look at Caesar; he rules over all these stinking apes because he's smart," Kyle said.

Lane breathed out a cloud of smoke and coughed a little. With a strange smile, he said, "Damn dirty apes."

"Caesar rules the same way we've tried to rule the Viet Cong." Tammy turned her head. "Look how that's gone down."

Jenny crinkled her face. "It's only a movie."

The joint completed the circle, ending up in Lane's hand. He held it aloft and said, "No, that's different. This reflects our own dystopian future through the prism of science fiction. Man is an ape."

Kyle chuckled. "That's heavy, man."

"We're doomed." Tammy sighed.

"That's not right." Jenny shook her head.

"Yeah, it is." Kyle took the smaller, resin-stained joint from Lane and yelled, "Hail Caesar, baby!"

Feeling lightheaded, Lane yelled, "Hail the Lawgiver!"

Jenny burst into laughter. "Hail Caesar!"

Tammy joined in. "Hail Nixon, the greatest ape of all!"

They all laughed harder than normal at the asinine joke under the influence of the grass. The ape warfare on screen sounded through the tinny speaker as smoke wafted out of the car and into the night.

Kyle snuffed out the roach in the ashtray. He moved in and said, "Hey, Jenny. Ape man wants a kiss."

"My ape man gets what he wants." Jenny positioned her body over the gearshift to get closer to Kyle.

"Damn right, baby!" Kyle kissed her gently.

Tammy grabbed hold of Lane's hand, keeping her eyes forward on the screen.

Feeling tired, Lane rested his head on her chest. "Those damn dirty apes." He yawned.

Tammy stroked his hair. "It's okay… Everything's okay."

 The sounds of the drive-in seemed far away. He opened his eyes and found himself under a starry night sky, standing in front of the Mobil Station, wearing his blue work coveralls with nothing underneath.

Inside the garage, Kyle, clad in coveralls with the zipper down, revealed his straining, greasy muscles as he tightened the header of his Challenger with a wrench. Kyle looked at Lane and pointed up to the metal sign.

Lane heard a ringing echo and followed the direction.

The painting of Pegasus shimmered, light shedding off its wings and white body. The commotion—the attempted flapping of feathers and the whinnying sound of a trapped, mythological horse—shook the sign. The sight shocked Lane with its surrealism.

Looking back down, Lane saw Kyle, his muscular pecs glistening against the moonlight as he turned and walked into the darkness of the garage—his car gone and forgotten.

"Hey, wait!" Lane yelled after him.

The strange Pegasus averted his eyes, and it was difficult not to look at the winged horse's attempt to escape. Light fell into pieces, melting into the ground on contact. Lane broke his gaze as it vanished.

Kyle was gone.

Out of the darkness, James appeared clad in unzipped work coveralls. Dirty and rough, his toned bare chest and happy trail only just visible, he walked forward, dangerous and sexy with his piercing blue eyes.

James smiled and said, "It's cool if you'd rather hang out with me, Lane."

EIGHT

THE WORDS FADED AS Lane came awake in the Challenger's backseat. Kyle shook him some more, and the car, parked on the curb in front of a suburban house, rocked a little from the motion.

Tammy and Jenny whispered on the sidewalk and laughed at the scene.

"Whoa... Whoa... What are you doing, man?" Lane breathed in sharply.

"Welcome back, little buddy," Kyle said, shaking Lane again.

"Alright already, I'm getting up." Lane shifted under Kyle's dominant proximity and pushed him away.

Kyle backed out of the car, smiling at the girls. "All's well, ladies."

"Hey, he fell asleep in my lap." Tammy stole a look at the windows of her house to see if a light was on. Softer, she said, "It was cute."

Lane got out and stood, stretching his sore back and neck. "How long was I out?"

"Maybe half an hour, cutie," Jenny said.

"You missed the end of the movie, but it's not a big deal since it wasn't as cool as the other ones," Kyle said.

"There were cool ones?" Tammy waited for the reaction.

"I like the apes. I must've been dog-tired." Lane rubbed the sleep out of his eyes.

"Second time you passed out today." Kyle smirked.

"Maybe I have narcolepsy or some rare disorder," Lane wondered aloud.

"You're a rarity, that's for sure." Tammy gave Lane a tight hug. "Goodnight, sleepy."

"I had a wonderful time." Jenny spoke to Kyle like they were alone.

"Me too," Kyle said softly, and he moved into her space. "Do you still want to go to the beach with us tomorrow?"

"What time?" Jenny asked, rising.

"Around noon, I guess," Kyle said.

"Yeah, that'll do," Jenny said, stepping up on her toes to kiss Kyle on the lips. It was so delicate it was almost imperceptible, but their bodies reacted to the connection like they were on fire.

Tammy looked from them to Lane and wrinkled her brow. "I really have to go to church in the morning."

"Sure you do." Lane feigned rejection.

"Maybe some other time," Tammy said, kissing Lane on the cheek. "You're a decent guy, Lane."

Looking down at the cracked pavement of the sidewalk, Lane said, "Goodnight, Tammy."

Kyle and Jenny parted lips in an air of youthful romance and thinly veiled teenage desire. He let her slip away as a light came on in the living room window of the green, cedar shake house and asked, "Where am I going to pick you up?"

"Meet me at Long John's. Melissa, Don, and some others are going to be there. We can all caravan to the beach together," Jenny said.

Kyle shrugged, showing little of his care. "Sounds good. See you, babe."

"Bye, Kyle," Jenny said and laughed. "Get some sleep, Lane." Smiling, she took Tammy's arm, and they walked up the front path.

The cracked, open door revealed a waiting shadow.

"Come on, Lane. Let's ride." Kyle punched Lane in the arm and halfway trotted around to the driver's side.

Lane looked at the girls as they giggled all the way through the front door. He sat in the passenger seat and saw that Kyle had that look he gets when he wants to say something but does not.

The car keys jingled in the silence.

"What?" Lane asked.

"Nothing, man." Kyle's jaw clenched.

"Why are you looking at me then?" Lane felt a little defensive.

Kyle cranked the key, and the engine rumbled with power. "You can be one strange cat, Lane."

"Hey, I can't help it. I'm drawn this way." Lane tapped his chest.

"Right on, man," Kyle said, punching the super-blue Challenger into gear. He still had that look, and Lane dreaded what words would come. Dreaded he'd have to lie, make excuses, and pretend to be someone else, else lose Kyle's friendship. "You want to go to the reservoir and finish the beer?"

"Sure, that'd be cool." Lane eased back into his seat, stifling a long, drawn-out sigh.

Kyle drove them to the freeway and the tension faded. "I'm going to let her out. Are you ready?"

"Hell yeah!" Lane felt the excitement of the coming rush.

Kyle drove up the ramp onto the freeway. The coast was clear, so he punched the gas and popped the clutch, shifting to fourth, then fifth.

The powerful engine vibrated the car's frame. Lane felt the force pushing him back deeper into the seat. Kyle laughed as they suddenly lurched forward. Speeding over one hundred thirty miles per hour, the road and countryside zoomed by, blurring together in a mosaic of streaking lights.

Lane laughed out loud with Kyle, who looked like a kid on a roller coaster. *There's nothing like this.* It was better than any pill or grass. *This is pure adrenaline—pure rush.*

"Oh shit! Hang on, there's our exit!" Kyle exclaimed.

Lane watched as the road sped by. *It's just me and Kyle, and no one can catch us.*

Kyle downshifted and turned the wheel sharply enough to skid. Somehow, he straightened out the tires in time to make the ramp. The muscle car stayed on the asphalt, almost hitting the embankment.

"That was freaking fantastic!" Lane rocked back and forth in his seat, feeling the best he had all day.

"Whew! No pigs out either." Kyle downshifted again, and the Challenger growled its steady rumble. "Damn, I'm good!"

"Fantastic," Lane said again as his rocking slowed.

Kyle felt full of pride and turned to a back road that followed the reservoir. He shut off the headlights and slowed to a hidden parking area.

"Nobody's here." Lane observed the darkened surroundings.

"The cops probably chased them off earlier, like they always do." Kyle stopped next to some overgrown weeds and shrubbery.

"I like it better this way." He really did. The dark of night, the emptiness, it made him feel at ease somehow.

Kyle set the brakes and opened his door. "The place is pretty cool to chill at when it is late like this."

Lane got out and took in the concrete and vine surroundings where the dirt road ended at the reservoir.

Ash, oaks, and Chinese tallow trees populated the edge of the industrial area, where cracked and dirty cement led down to a small, debris-filled stream. Its trickling sound was soothing under the star-filled night sky.

Kyle opened the trunk, scooping up the last four beers in his hands, and said, "Perfect, two each."

Lane took two cans of beer. "Let's lie on the side so we can see the stars."

"I dig it. That sounds really chill." Kyle led them down the side to a clear space with a view of swirling galaxies and the crescent moon in the west.

Lane enjoyed the moment because the humidity seemed low for a change and the mosquitoes were few.

Sprawling out, Kyle made his body as comfortable as possible on the rough surface. "This is far out."

Lane lay back next to him, staring intently at the night sky as Kyle closed his eyes. Lane noticed a starlike object glowing across the heavens and said, "Check it out."

"What's that?" Kyle stirred.

"Do you see that moving speck of light?" Lane asked.

"Where?" Kyle eyed the sky.

"Look." Lane pointed out the spot. "You see it?"

"Aw yeah." Kyle watched it move. "What is that, a UFO?"

"I think it might be Skylab. NASA is going to fix it, but they might not," Lane said.

"Far out." Kyle put his arms back and cradled the back of his head. "What's wrong with it?"

"I think it's falling out of orbit," Lane said, copying Kyle's position as he watched the sky. Just the two of them, drinking beer and staring out at the stars. Lane wished it could always be this way.

"You mean Skylab might crash?" Kyle asked.

"Nah." Lane shrugged. "Well, it might."

"It sounds better than getting nuked." Kyle smiled, watching Skylab cross the sky.

"True." Lane smiled too. "We'd be dead either way."

"It ain't going to happen." Kyle shook his head and smirked. "It'll probably crash into the ocean."

"No, they'll fix it. NASA is amazing." Lane lifted himself up on his elbows and beamed. "I always wanted to be an astronaut."

"You're from the Heights." Kyle laughed again. "There's no way."

"I still dream about it, though." Lane breathed out and lowered himself back down. "It'd be so cool to be up there, away from all this."

"Hell, I'd settle on driving west and never looking back," Kyle said, wistful.

"Me too." Lane felt the vastness of space. "I just want to go far away and live life."

"Having no money keeps me stuck here. I just can't get ahead," Kyle said.

"I have to dream, man." Lane sighed, feeling alone inside. "It's all I got."

Kyle drank his beer in silence, lost in his own thoughts.

Lane was near, but his mind was far away as he watched Skylab cross the astral plane. *If I were an astronaut, I could be a hero. Down here, I'm nobody. I'm just a gas jockey with a crush on his best friend. There has to be something better than this.*

PART TWO

TRICKED

NINE

Outside the house on Lamar Drive, the bespectacled teenager brushed his bangs out of his eyes and started the red Plymouth GTX. He revved it once, liking the deep sound of its engine. He glanced at the house and breathed out as he put the gear in reverse.

Faint music played from a transistor radio inside the hazy living room of the house. The handcuffs clicked on the scruffy teenager's wrists, and he showed how tight they were. Without giving away the secret, he moved his cuffed hands around until the lock popped open and they were free.

"Now you try it." The scruffy teenager dangled the handcuffs innocently.

"I don't know," another teenage boy said, leaning back on the couch. He was dubious and doubtful as he hooked a finger in the blue paisley bandana tied around his neck.

"You saw how simple it is," he said, calm and casual.

The teenage boy put the cuffs on his wrists. He wriggled his wrist one way and another. The handcuff trick looked easy. Perplexed, the boy could not figure it out. "How did you do it?"

"With this." The scruffy teenager flashed the key and pocketed it.

"You got me, man." He gave a short, throaty laugh. "Now let me out," the boy said, not liking the change in vibe.

The scruffy teenager shook his head.

Stoned, the boy laughed nervously until the man with burning eyes walked into the living room. The handcuffs clinked, not loosening but tightening. The smile vanished. "Who is he?" the boy asked, frightened.

"This is his house—his rules," the scruffy one said, then stepped back to let the stranger appraise the boy.

"I've been waiting for you," the man said with relish. He had a working-class look with short, dark curly hair and seemed like anyone else in their thirties, except his eyes were too intense.

The boy tried to run but tripped and fell. It all seemed unreal. An iron grip locked onto his leg, and the man dragged him toward the hallway. The boy screamed. The haunting organ opening of Deep Purple's "Child in Time" raised in volume as the scruffy teenager picked up the transistor radio and followed them, humming along to the song.

"Don't do this!" The hallway floor slid by as the teenage boy twisted and turned, dragged into the backroom. "Please, let me go!"

He kicked and thrashed about, but the scruffy teenager held his legs as the man yanked him up to a board. Exposed loose ropes hung from holes cut through each side. There were bloodstains and scratches on the wood. On the floor beside it was an open toolbox and some glass rods. The rope slid through the handcuffs, and the boy panicked as it pulled taut, stretching his arms.

"Now, I'm gonna have me some fun." The man reached into the toolbox, his eyes on fire.

The scruffy teenager watched with an abstracted gaze, turning up the transistor's volume. The singer on the radio screamed as the song became more manic, and the boy screamed too as the knife cut into his flesh.

PART THREE

HIGH ISLAND

THE VIEW OF EARTH *from outer space was awe-inspiring. Lane watched Skylab catch fire as it entered the atmosphere from the rotating, orbiting platform of the space station he was on. It was a beautiful sight as it streaked down, leaving a trail of flame in its wake.*

Lane smiled, checking his reflection in the transparent wall, a blue coverall spacesuit with a logo of the planet and stars over his heart. The floor moved with the rotation of the station as the doomed Skylab ebbed out of sight, sinking into the swirling chaos of the clouds that swam above the oceans far below.

The metallic echo of footsteps filled the slow-spinning corridor. Someone wearing gravity boots was approaching. Lane pulled free a boot of his own and turned to see the other astronaut with familiar dark hair and piercing, ice-blue eyes.

Lane beamed at his comrade. "You missed it, James. Skylab is going down in flames, like Icarus falling from the sun."

James looked out at the Earth below as it moved out of view, revealing the dark vastness of space. "The fall from the heavens is vast."

Lane looked at James, unease filling his heart. "What does that mean?"

"Pay attention, Lane. It's coming." James reached out and grabbed Lane's shoulder to emphasize its importance.

"I don't understand," Lane said, touching James's hand.

"You will." James's eyes swirled like a crystal blue ocean as he said, "Believe me, you will."

A meteor hit the station, and it shuddered and shook. The impact knocked it out of orbit, and the transparent viewing wall cracked into an ever-growing web until it shattered. Air rushed out.

Lane tried to hang on to James, but the force was strong. "James, what's happening?"

"The chaos is here now," James said, smiling the smile of one who knew the way.

"I'm afraid. I don't want—" Lane felt the pull, and he grabbed on tight to James.

In a rush of breaking sounds, the depressurization sucked them out together into space, followed by silence as they floated amongst the stars.

Content at last, peace filled Lane. He matched James's serene smile with one of his own. Then in a flash, peace vanished, and their smiles faded as the space station imploded into a black hole, bringing a deep, dark fear of the unknown.

Ten

WHAT A TRIP! LANE woke in a sweat, anxious and unsure of where he was for a moment beyond the vivid dream. The bedroom was like a sauna, high in humidity. He pulled back the bedsheet and scratched his balls through his white boxers.

I still feel like I'm floating.

He stumbled as he stepped to the window. At first, it would not budge, and he strained until it broke free, bringing in some fresh air. Outside, the sun was beating down, with the temperature already passing eighty degrees.

It's a perfect day for the beach. He glanced at the people hanging out by the pool. *Those poor dopes. I'm so glad I get to split out of here.*

He rummaged through his wooden drawers, knocking over a couple of records in search of shorts. All he could find was an old pair of school gym shorts that were red and way too short. Reluctant, he tossed them on the bed. He also found a clean shirt and an oversized beach towel with an image of shady palms in its stitching, and he added them to the pile.

Lane pulled on the solid gray T-shirt and slid into yesterday's jeans, which were always decent for a couple of days. One of the fallen records caught his eye, and he clicked on the player, sliding the vinyl into the groove. Townes Van Zandt's voice broke into a folksy tune with "Blue Ridge Mountains" from the album *High, Low, and In Between*.

He found some sandals under the bed and bundled them up in the towel with the shorts. Checking his pockets, he discovered keys and a leather wallet with a jagged piece of paper sticking out of the fold.

The white napkin had James and 946-2302 written in neat pen strokes.

Lane held it up in the sunlight, and pieces of his strange dream swirled inside his mind. *I should call James. I have to be careful, but I can't shake him.*

He slid the paper back inside his wallet and shoved it into his jeans pocket, then he swept the loose change off of the corner of the dresser into the palm of his hand. The bedroom door creaked when opened; it always did. Lane hated that, and he cringed as he left his room.

The living room was dark, with heavy cotton sheets in place of curtains. Kyle lay asleep, sprawled out on his twin bed on top of the sheets. He twisted to the side, causing one sheet to wrap around his leg and expose his bulging underwear.

Lane took another step and paused.

Kyle stirred. Eyes halfway opened, he sleepily asked, "What time is it, man?"

"It's after eleven. We got to get going soon," Lane said.

"Twenty more minutes, and I'm up." Kyle drifted back into slumber, turning over on his side.

Lane broke his stare and grabbed his boots by the door. He took them in hand and went out onto the small porch walkway to put them on.

Some kids splashed around the pool under the supervision of their young mother and a couple of older guys who were drinking beer and barbecuing. The sweet aroma of steaks grilling filled Lane's nostrils and caused his stomach to growl.

The payphone, bolted onto a brownish, red brick wall of the Ben Hur Apartment building, faced the gated pool, close to the gravel parking lot. Lane dug some dimes out of his jeans pocket and plopped one in the phone slot. The receiver felt warm to the touch. He spun his finger around the rotary dial seven times, then listened to the faraway ringing from the ear speaker.

"Wallace speaking," a curt voice announced through the receiver.

"Hey, man, this is Lane," Lane said over another splash from the pool.

"What did I do to deserve a morning call from you, son?" Wallace sounded pleased.

"I know. I know." Lane twisted the cord. "I only call when I want something."

"So, what do you want?" Wallace asked.

"Can we borrow your ice chest?" Lane asked and added, "We're going to the beach, and cold beer is better than hot and sandy beer, if you know what I mean."

"Sure is." Wallace laughed his dog-throated sailor laugh. "You know where to find me."

"Cool. We'll be by in a bit." Before Lane could hang up, the loud dial tone erupted in his ear.

Lane cradled the receiver in one hand and pulled out the ragged napkin with James's number. In the sunlight, the ink-written digits looked slightly smeared. He took a breath, looked at the kids splashing in the pool, and plugged in another dime.

"Here goes nothing." One drawn-out ring followed another. Lane considered hanging up, but before he could, someone picked up the call.

"Hello!" an irate voice lashed out.

"Hello, is James in?" Lane asked meekly.

"It's a little too early to be calling. I work nights and don't have time for this crap," James's father said in a diatribe.

"I'm sorry. I thought it was cool to call after ten." Lane hoped the bitter man would not hang the phone up on him.

"That's during the week, but this is my freaking day off!" James's father spat the words out.

"Will you tell him Lane called?" Lane asked, dreading the answer.

"Hang on." The sound of yelling caused static in the receiver, and the only thing he could make out was, "James, get your sorry ass out here!"

Lane sighed, shifting his feet and drumming his fingers on the black telephone box.

"Hello?" James's familiar voice said in a strange tone.

"Hey, this is Lane." Lane felt his pulse rise.

"Lane." James's voice softened and brightened. "Right... You called!"

"I told you I would," Lane said.

"Is this about the beach?" James asked.

"Yeah." Lane paused, then asked, "You still wanna go?"

"Right on." James also paused, the awkwardness bleeding through the phone, then said, "Of course I do."

"Where do you live?" Lane asked.

"On 23rd Street, just off Rutland, it's the second house from the corner, the one with the beat-up truck out front," James explained.

"Cool, we'll swing by in a few and come get you," Lane said in a rush.

"I got some ludes leftover." With a hint of slyness, James asked, "Should I bring them?"

"How many is that?" Lane wondered where the day was going to take them.

"Five or six," James said. "I guess."

"Can you hook up Kyle and his chick?" Land tapped the phone box.

"I can do that, as long as we get a couple apiece to chill," James said.

"Me and you?" Lane wondered aloud, taken aback.

"Yeah, it'll be chaos," James said infectiously.

"I can dig it." A smile crept onto Lane's face.

"See you soon, Lane." James breathed during the pause.

"See you, James." Lane put the handle on the cradle. He had a fleeting memory of his strange dream and the vortex of space, and James's voice echoed in his mind. *The chaos is here now.*

Should I tell James about the dream? Lane smiled to himself, feeling good. After last night's ordeal with Tammy grilling him and the tricks of his weird subconscious, the dream made it all worthwhile.

Another splash broke over the side of the pool as a boy did a cannonball dive, to his mother's frown.

Lane's thoughts returned to the moment as he quickened his step and bound up the stairs two at a time.

Inside the apartment, Kyle surprised him—dressed and ready to go.

"I thought you were crashing," Lane said.

"Nah, I can't keep Jenny waiting." Kyle pocketed his billfold. "I told her we would be at Long John's by noon, and it's eleven thirty."

"Cool. Can we grab the ice chest from Old Man Wallace?" Lane asked.

"Sure, we can get the beer and only be a little late," Kyle said.

"One other thing," Lane said, biting his lip.

"What's that?" Kyle reached for his keys on the card table.

"Is it cool if we swing by and pick up James?" Lane asked.

"James?" Kyle paused mid-motion, dumbfounded. "You want us to pick up the guy from last night?"

"Yeah, he's cool." Lane shrugged.

"I don't know the cat that well, man." Kyle shook his head no.

"He has some ludes." Lane tilted his head.

Kyle's mood brightened. "Oh, well, that's a different story."

Lane could not help smiling.

"He's not far, right?" Kyle asked.

"Just down the street," Lane said.

"Cool, but he better not be trouble, or I'll leave him there," Kyle warned.

"No trouble." Lane smacked his chest. "I vouch for him."

"What the hell are you, a tough guy?" Kyle playfully punched Lane in the arm.

"Screw off, man." Lane moved to punch back, but changed his mind.

"They better be real." Kyle flexed. "That's all I am saying."

"I said screw off, Kyle." Lane threw a punch at Kyle's shoulder, but he turned, and it hit him in the chest instead.

"You're dead now," Kyle said, lunging.

Lane ran, only just avoiding Kyle's hulking frame. He darted to his room and swooped down to grab his stuff—all folded up in the towel. Lane rushed to make it back out, but Kyle grabbed him, forcing him down.

Kyle laughed at him. "What are you going to do, little man?"

"Get off me!" Lane squirmed underneath, trying to free himself from the bear hold, but could not overcome Kyle's strength.

"Come on, make me." Kyle powered down, holding back Lane's arms.

Lane struggled and felt weak. "Enough, Kyle. You know I'm claustrophobic."

"Oh, yeah." Kyle held Lane down harder. "What are you going to do?"

"I'm going to get you for this," Lane said, out of breath.

"It ain't gonna happen," Kyle smirked, smug in his control.

"Let me up!" Lane hollered.

Kyle got up, leaving Lane on the floor. "Come on, we got to go."

"Dammit, Kyle!" Catching his breath, Lane looked up at a dominant Kyle. He took the offered hand, wheezing from the exertion. "You're lucky I like you."

"I will show you a couple of things one day," Kyle said, lifting Lane up off the floor with one arm.

"Like what?" Lane asked, curious about what rough things he could show him.

"I could teach you how to defend yourself." Kyle slapped Lane on the shoulder. "You need to know how to fight, boy."

"That would be cool," Lane said, finding something new to admire in Kyle.

"Let's get out of here." Kyle grabbed his keys off the card table and walked toward the door.

"Alrighty, let me grab my shorts." Lane scurried off.

"Hurry up." Kyle called after him. "I'll be in the car!"

"Okay!" Lane hollered as he grabbed his things off the floor, rolling the towel over them in a small bundle.

The hiss of static from the record player drew his attention as the needle stayed stuck in the last groove, round and round. Lane adjusted it and clicked the off switch. His eyes darted about the room, and then he was out of the apartment, locking the door behind him.

The mom and kids had abandoned the swimming pool, leaving puddles and wet footprints on the cement. The smell of the barbecue taunted Lane, reminding him to eat before a day of drinking, while the roar of the Challenger greeted him in the gravel lot.

"It's going to be one hot day, man!" Kyle smiled and punched the accelerator to peel out the tires.

Lane's lips involuntarily parted into a smile. He loved the moment of the muscle car's power and speed on the road. He tuned the radio, and wavy static cleared into voices.

"This is KPRC 950 AM, and we are covering the rise in runaway youth. Caller, you are on."

"My son did not runaway like some juvenile delinquent. He went to the grocery store and never came home. Something happened, and the police do not—"

"Who's been messing with my buttons?" Kyle clicked to FM, and Mick Jagger's voice, belting out "Angie", filled the air.

"Don't look at me. I just turned it on." Lane sighed and said, "They play this song too much."

"Hey, it's a cool song." Kyle cranked up the volume.

Lane felt the breeze hit his face as he watched the light dilly-dally through the trees above as they raced down 27th Street in record time. The muscle car screeched to a halt, cut short before it could really open up. The 383 engine rumbled heavily as it idled. Wallace sat on his porch in the same worn-out swing, watching the neighborhood over his morning beer.

"I'll be right back." Lane jumped out of the car and bounded across the yard.

"That boy is going to crash that fancy hot rod one day," Wallace said.

"I hope it's not today," Lane said with a lopsided grin and asked, "How are you doing?"

"Like the weather," Wallace said. "I'm in my dog days."

"You're one salty dog," Lane said with a grin.

Wallace swallowed a mouthful of beer. "No one has put this old dog down yet."

Lane laughed. "I ain't taking you to the pound, Wallace, because we're going to the beach."

"The chest is on the side of the porch, over there," Wallace said, pointing. "I already iced it up for you."

"Cool." Lane grabbed the red Coleman chest by the metal handle, letting it hang from one hand. "Thanks."

"Lane, stop by this week," Wallace said, turning serious. "I want to show you something."

Kyle honked the horn three times in quick succession, mirroring his impatience.

Looking at Wallace, antsy but curious, Lane asked, "What's that?"

"Come by, and you'll see," Wallace said.

Why can't people just say what's on their mind? "Alrighty, I'll bring back your chest after work tomorrow or the next day," Lane said.

"Sounds good. Y'all better be safe out there," Wallace said.

"We will." Lane wondered what was up, but there was no time to dig. He waved off Wallace and walked on.

Kyle revved up the Challenger with urgency. The trunk was already open, and the car was facing the opposite way. Lane heaved the ice chest into the trunk and leaned against the car for a second to catch his breath. Across the way, the Henley house caught his eye with its drawn drapes, and he remembered the teenage boy smoking a joint in the backseat of the dark red GTX.

How are Wayne Henley and his crowd so bad? Everyone parties.

Something felt off, though—something about the boy's eyes.

"Come on, man!" Kyle honked again and Lane slammed the trunk closed.

He was barely in the passenger seat when the car took off, the force pushing him back in his seat.

"Where to?" Kyle asked as he sped up.

"Oh." Lane closed his eyes and said, "James lives on 23rd at Rutland."

"Good, it's close. Hang on." Kyle punched it, shifting gears like a pro racer.

"Wahoo!" Lane yelled, feeling the adrenaline rush.

Kyle skidded the Challenger on Rutland, the wheels almost coming off the road. He maintained the balance as they raced the four blocks in a couple of blinks of the eye.

"It's to the right!" Lane yelled.

"Got it." Kyle downshifted and cut the wheel sharp, avoiding the small drainage ditches that lined the front of the houses.

"Stop here!" Lane yelled again.

Kyle slammed on the brakes. The smell of burnt rubber was thick and acrid in the hot, humid air. "Hurry up! We still got to get beer."

"Hold your horses. I don't know his parents." Lane shook off the whiplash.

"Just hurry, Lane." Kyle pressed the buttons on the radio, searching for another station but returning to KLOL to wait out a commercial break.

"Chill, and I'll be quick." Out of the car, Lane felt his balance was a little off from the high-speed venture.

James's house was like many others in the neighborhood: a small bungalow with weathered paint and a weedy yard in need of mowing. The promised beat-up truck, a rusted, once-red '55 Ford F100, rested in the driveway with the look of something that had not moved in a while.

The heatwave of summer was in full effect. Lane sweated as he walked up the cracked sidewalk to the front door. He felt eyes on him from inside. Closer, he heard scuffling along with the low murmur of voices. Lane jumped despite himself as Kyle blasted the car horn.

Cursing under his breath, he reached out to knock on the door. It opened, and he saw James's cool blue eyes gazing upon him. He could not help but smile. James's clothes were similar to his—jeans and a T-shirt, with a bundled towel at his side.

James stepped out fast and shut the door behind him. "Let's get out of here."

"Sure, something wrong?" Lane asked.

"Nah, just the usual family fun." James's eyes darted to the door.

Kyle blasted the horn again, causing them both to jump.

James's old man stepped out of the house. A too-small, dirty muscle shirt clung to his hefty torso. "Where the hell do you think you're going with those punks?" Wispy black hair covered beefy arms that belied the muscle underneath as the man raised a finger and pointed.

"Nowhere." James looked down, and continued, "But we might go down to the beach to get some sun."

His father leered. "Nowhere is exactly where you're going."

"I'll see you later, Dad." James grabbed Lane by the arm and steered him towards the car.

"If you walk away from me, you can't come back to my house." His father raised his voice. "You understand me?"

"Not now." James shook his head, walking backwards. "I'll talk to you later."

"If you're living under my roof, you follow my goddamn rules." His father made a fist. "Now get over here, boy."

"Come on, Lane. Hurry up," James urged Lane toward the car. "He's in a mood."

Kyle honked the horn again for good measure.

James's old man turned red, whipped off his belt, and came at them with menace.

"Oh shit, get in the car!" Lane reacted to the change and shoved James into the backseat.

James's father was pounding on the car door just as it shut. "Open that goddamn door right now and get out here and face me like a man!"

"He better not mess my car up," Kyle said, his teeth gritted.

James shook Kyle's seat. "Drive, man! Drive!"

"What's his problem?" Kyle laughed, despite the tension. "I swear if he leaves a mark, someone's going to pay."

James caught Kyle's eye in the rearview mirror and opened and closed his mouth.

"Come on, Kyle. Let's get out of here," Lane urged. He felt uncomfortable with less than a quarter-inch of glass separating him from the raging man outside.

"That's it, James! Don't you dare come back tonight! You are no longer welcome here!" James's father spat the words out, the veins bulging in his neck.

Kyle laughed as he hit the gas pedal. Turning the steering wheel, he scared the man. "Screw you, you old goat!"

In the backseat, James looked from Lane to his raging father, then back in awe. Kyle peeled the tires out, tearing up the gravel. The muscle car spun out, and they left the man in a cloud of dust while he was cursing up a storm.

"That was wrong." Lane laughed and looked back to see how James was reacting.

James smiled a weary smile and asked, "Is it okay if I crash with you tonight?"

"Sure, it's cool," Lane blurted out without thinking. "I mean, there's no way you can go back now."

Kyle gave a warning look, then shrugged. "You can crash in Lane's room because I'm bringing Jenny back."

Genuinely interested, Lane asked, "You think so?"

"Today is going to be the day, man." Kyle smirked, gripping the wheel.

"What are you going to do once you get it?" Lane asked.

"I don't know." Kyle glanced in the rearview mirror. "What do you mean?"

"You're going to be bored and ready for the next chick," Lane said.

"Hey, man, I'm not that guy," Kyle said.

Lane shrugged with a "whatever you say" look.

"Well, I'm not *always* that guy. Dammit, Lane." Kyle punched Lane in the arm.

"Hey, guys, thanks for rescuing me," James said, speaking up from the backseat.

"No problem," Lane mumbled. He didn't want to be too keen.

The Challenger checked its shocks as its right tire hit a pothole. James breathed out. "I should've sneaked out."

Rocking back and forth in his seat from the impact, Lane said, "You got to get away from your old man or you'll lose it."

James caught his eye and nodded.

Gripping the wheel as he turned onto Heights Boulevard, Kyle merged into mild traffic. "Hey, James, you bring those pills?"

"Yeah, man." James pulled out a small plastic bag with six blue capsules. "Check it out."

Kyle sneaked a look and grinned. "Alright, that's what I'm talking about."

Touching the bag, feeling the smoothness of a pill through the plastic, Lane nodded in approval. "The beach will be flying."

James put away his stash and leaned back in the back seat, relaxing. "Yeah, it will."

ELEVEN

On a slow cruise, the Challenger entered the Rice Food Market parking lot off Studewood Street to amble down an aisle. Fresh lines marked the pavement, although the asphalt had sprouted cracks from the summer heat. Kyle found a space to the side to avoid the shopping cart habits of careless moms. Getting out of the car, he took the lead, with Lane and James in tow. They walked past the few cars in the lot, which was normal for a church morning.

Kyle pushed the heavy glass and steel door open. The store was fair-sized, but it seemed like its heyday had passed. A bored middle-aged cashier, whose beauty had faded along with her options, looked them over with disdain. He led them to the beer section and passed back a couple of cases to the boys.

"Lone Star, Kyle? Why always Lone Star?" Feeling the weight of the cases in his arms, Lane asked, "Can we just get Bud like we did last night?"

"Simple. It's cheap, and we can get a lot more," Kyle said.

"Hell, it doesn't matter after the first couple anyway," James chimed in.

"Don't help." Lane sighed. "It's my money."

"I'll chip in some dollars," James offered.

"Cool." Lane caught himself staring and looked down at the beer.

Kyle shrugged. "I'll get y'all back on payday."

Lane relented, feeling a little used and knowing full well Kyle wasn't going to pay up—ever. "Alright, quantity then."

They carried the cases to the clerk's empty checkout lane. She was shaking her head back and forth before they got there.

"What's the matter?" Kyle asked. A flash of anger crossed his eyes.

"According to the Blue Law, we cannot sell beer until after twelve o'clock on Sundays," the cashier said, meeting his stare.

Kyle looked at the clock above the tall glass window walls that made up the front of the store. "That's only five minutes!"

"Then you have to wait," she said with a click of her tongue.

"You've got to be kidding me." Kyle was furious.

"Next in line, please," the cashier said, looking past Kyle's shoulder.

Kyle muttered under his breath, "Bitch."

"Did you say something?" The cashier was unsure if she heard right.

"I said, I got an itch." Kyle glared, set the beer on the floor, and scratched his crotch before heading outside.

Alongside James, Lane chuckled, then turned on his puppy-dog look. "Will you watch our stuff, ma'am? Until it's time?"

"I can't promise you anything." The cashier was icy now.

James got closer. "You're such a doll."

The cashier shifted, unsure if it was a compliment or not, and said, "I can get the next in line."

An exasperated lady with rollers in her hair wheeled up her cart while scolding her kids. "No, Jimmy. You know they don't sell toys on Sunday, so put the jacks back."

Lane elbowed James and said, "The Blue Law is such a joke; it must be a Texas thing because it just doesn't make a lick of sense."

"Aren't the church and state supposed to be separate?" James adjusted one case, slipping under his arm as he set it down.

"The fat cats and morality police piss all over us every chance they get." Lane opened the door with his foot.

The bright sunlight blinded them for a moment.

"Yeah, man, the Heights is the armpit of the city," James said as he leaned on a wall.

"It shouldn't be a crime to buy a toy on Sunday." Lane sighed.

"That's no lie," James said.

Lane noticed a small boy wearing a brown and tan ringer shirt with a sparkly *Scooby Doo* patch and dirty bare feet. A yellow '70 Chevy van with tinted windows pulled up, blocking Lane's view.

"Everything we do for fun is a crime," James said in defiance.

"Then screw it. I guess we're criminals," Lane replied, staring at the van.

"Right on, man. Criminals. I like the sound of it; it reminds me of outlaws in a biker gang." James's smile lit up.

"That's a righteous trip there!" Lane looked over the lot. He saw Kyle light up a cigarette and pace around his shiny, blue Challenger, looking for imperfections.

James followed his gaze. "What's up with him?"

"Oh, he only smokes and fidgets like that when he's mad. He's probably checking out if your dad did any damage. He'll cool out in a bit, but never say a word about it," Lane said.

"Have you known him for a long time?" James tilted his head.

"A couple of years," Lane said wistfully. "We used to play ball in the neighborhood, at least until we started smoking grass."

James laughed. "That ought to do it."

Lane watched the van drive off, and something seemed wrong—dirty bare feet on the hot asphalt—but he could not figure out why. He saw a boy wearing a tan shirt with his mother in curlers scolding him, and he was unsure if it was the same one.

James jabbed him in the chest. "Come back to Earth, space ranger."

"Sorry, I was just thinking," Lane said, snapping out of his daze.

"You're one strange cat," James said, staring at Lane long enough for them to lock eyes.

"Funny,"—Lane held the stare, his heart hammering—"we said the same thing about you last night."

James, with a curious look on his face, was about to reply when Kyle walked up.

"Let's get this over with," Kyle said as he led the way again.

The building looked like a sailor's cabin with its purposefully aged wood. Rocks abutted it like a ship docked on land, surrounded by the smell of grease and seafood. Heavy rope lined the walkway to the building, making it a gangway of sorts in the summer breeze. On the hanging sign, a pirate with a parrot on his shoulder swung below the words Long John Silver's Sea Food Shoppe.

The parking lot seemed fairly packed with a few muscle cars and work trucks. On the back of the lot rested a dusty green '68 El Camino, parked next to a dumpster, and some tall pampas grass. Kyle parked the Challenger on the opposite side, where there were no cars next to his chosen spot.

Lane opened his door, entranced by the El Camino. He held the seat to let James out, then poked him in the side. "Look over there. That's it... That's that kid Jamie's car."

"It sure is, man. That's kind of creepy." James's grin grew, and he said, "Maybe his body is in the trash next to it."

"Don't weird me out," Lane said as he observed the scene, getting a chill.

A greenish-yellow pollen had collected on top of the windshield of the El Camino, where it had fallen from a late-blooming Chinese tallow tree above it.

"Hey, I'm just saying that it's odd that the car is still here." James shrugged, enjoying the moment.

"Quit yammering and let's go inside." Kyle moved them onward.

"Chill out already. Jenny is in there, waiting with the gang. She ain't run off on you." Lane airily tapped Kyle on the shoulder. "Not yet."

Kyle glowered and chewed on the inside of his jaw.

"We should check inside the dumpster." James took a tentative step forward.

"I'm not going over there." Lane stood his ground.

"Jamie is probably somewhere out in the sun. Now, let's go eat so we can get to the beach sometime today," Kyle said, putting an end to the discussion and walking up the gangway toward a heavy wood and glass-pane door.

"Come on, James. Let it go." Lane urged. "I'm starving."

"Y'all are no fun," James said, pulling himself away from the dark idea and falling in line.

Inside, the restaurant had the feel of a ship's galley. Aside from the large windows in front, the rest were smaller portholes. More heavy rope lined the way to the order counter, with the minimal crew dressed as seaworthy as fast food allowed.

The gang, spread out over two booths, laughed at a punchline to an unheard story. Blond, all-American Troy and his raven-haired girl, Angie, held court with lifeguard Don and (too hot for him) Melissa in one, and the other booth held Tammy's older brother Ted, mousy Sally, and the lovely, doe-eyed Jenny.

The heavy wooden door slammed with a bang, and Kyle rang the captain's bell, drawing the group's attention.

Jenny was up on her feet in an instant. "Kyle, it's about time you made it."

"I'm sorry, babe. I forgot about the damn Blue Law, and we had to wait until noon to get the beer," Kyle said, catching Jenny with an arm.

"I am glad you did, buddy." Troy smiled and nodded. "All I brought was a bottle of Jack and some—"

Angie gave a disapproving look. "Something for us, Troy."

"Hey, I've got some cases of beer in my trunk too!" Ted exclaimed, and a vein pulsed out of his pale forehead. He looked similar to Tammy, with red hair, but he was big and muscular.

Don made a goofy face, half-smile, half-drug-induced haze. "And I got more of that magic grass."

"Who are your friends, Kyle?" Melissa twisted her tan body, and her green bikini top was visible through her open shirt.

Kyle looked at her chest, then darted his eyes back up to her face. "Lane, back here is my roommate, and this is James."

Lane watched James shake hands with Melissa, holding her hand a little too long. He looked away, feeling self-conscious with Ted and Sally in the mix.

James jumped into the center of things with a question: "What was the story when we walked in?"

"Oh yeah, we were just kidding about Tony." Troy laughed again.

"Tony used to be cool, man." Don tried to defend his friend. "He lives next door to me. I've always known that kid."

"So, what happened?" James pressed.

"We were sitting in class a couple of months ago, and you can see behind the cafeteria from the science room." Troy went on until Angie took over.

"Tony was with some other guy, most likely Mike, huffing from a brown paper bag, thinking they were out of sight," Angie said, breathless and excited.

Melissa broke in. "Those two losers were hyperventilating, playing the pass-out game."

"What's the pass-out game?" Lane inquired.

"It's where someone takes a huff of paint or glue and holds it in. Another person then grabs them by their face, covering their nose and mouth, until they pass out and have a tripped-out dream."

Don looked around at the gang and lost his smile. "At least that's what people tell me."

"Those heads were totally oblivious. Mr. Grant, the vice principal, walked up behind them while they were huffing. He yelled something, and they ran. It was a riot. They kept tripping and falling down. Their jerky movements reminded me of the *Keystone Cops* in one of those old silent films. Damn, they must've been high." Troy faintly smiled but felt the second telling was not as cool as the first.

"Tony ran right into the fence, and the prom banner came loose, wrapping around his face," Sally said. She snorted, and the others laughed. "He kept pulling at it. Her face..." Sally snorted two more times. "Her face covered his. He looked like the homecoming queen."

"What a loser, man," Ted said, more to himself than to the gang.

"Well, the homecoming queen gets around." Melissa laughed.

Kyle settled in with Jenny and turned to Lane with some dollars. "Hey, go get us some food."

"What the hell, Kyle?" Lane threw up his hands. "You have money now?"

"I found some in a stray pocket." Kyle shrugged and ordered. "Anyway, go get a treasure chest for me and my girl."

Lane snatched the money and nodded at Kyle. "Alright, anybody else want anything?"

Ted and Sally shook their heads while listening to their friends in the other booth talk about surfing. Angie and Melissa nodded, while Troy and Don were all dreamy-eyed about the potential waves.

"I want some fish and chips," James said, angling for a seat.

"Whoa, you're coming with me then," Lane said, grabbing James's sleeve.

"Sure thing, mister," James said, tagging after Lane. "And some hush puppies."

Lane smiled and pretended to ignore James while walking past an oddly placed wooden ship's wheel, its spokes set amidst some rope netting on the walls.

A sign on the counter of a pirate with a knife between his teeth displayed the captain's orders: Get Your Eats Before You Get Your Seats!

The Long John's crewman was pimply and young, with a distracted look in his eye, belying his age of about sixteen. "What's doing?"

"Not much. Can I get two orders of fish and chips, a treasure chest, and three drinks?" Lane asked.

"And an order of hush puppies," James insisted.

"Do you want the three or the six?" The crewman asked in monotone.

"Six ought to do it." Lane turned to James, who shrugged. Past him, he could see the green El Camino out the porthole, sitting desolate in the lot. "Hey, did you know the kid who owns the El Camino outside?"

The teenager looked at Lane like he was an alien. "Jamie left. That's all." Nervous, the boy picked at his face. "Look, your food will be out in a few minutes. That will be four seventy-eight."

"Here you go." Lane watched the young crewman fidget with the register, then he looked through the porthole outside and felt a weird vibe.

"That car has got you spooked," James said, reeling Lane back into the moment.

"I don't know, man. I feel there is something I should know, something that's out of place," Lane said.

"How so, Lane?" James wondered.

Lane's eyes moved to James, and he said, "It's like trying to remember something, and I almost grasp it, but it slips away."

"Like sands on the beach. That's poetry, man." James smiled, but his eyes sought the window.

"Here you go. I got you Cokes." The clerk slid the tan drink cups, with pirate treasure maps on their sides, across the slick countertop. "I hope that's cool."

"No worries, you got it right." Lane passed James a drink while sipping the sweet carbonation from another one. He pulled away from the counter, leaned on the wooden railing behind them, and looked James in the eyes. "Whenever it comes to me, I'll tell you."

"Cool," James said, tasting his soda. He looked Lane over, appraising him. "You know what strikes me as strange?"

"What's that?" Lane asked.

"I've never seen you in school before. We live in the same neighborhood, and I haven't seen you." James tilted his head.

"That's no secret." Lane held his gaze steady. "I dropped out when I was sixteen."

"How come?" James seemed surprised. "You seem smart—hell, smarter than me."

"My mom's sick. I tried to keep up in school, and it worked for a while, until it didn't." Lane looked down. "We lost the house when she went to the hospital."

"I'm sorry, man." James bit his lip. "What happened to her?"

"They don't know. Something was bleeding in her brain. They're running tests." Lane looked back up. "It's been over two months."

"Is that how long you and Kyle have been roommates?" James asked.

"Yep. I wish I could leave it all behind, but I guess I got to see it through," Lane said.

"That's honorable." James half-smiled. "I don't know if I'd do that for anyone in my family."

"What's your family like?" Lane asked, interested. "Besides the old man, I mean."

"Besides him? The usual family stuff, I guess. My mom keeps to herself. She always says she's going to leave my dad—take Jan and Theresa and run—but she never will." James stopped with a question. "You don't have any brothers or sisters, do you?"

"Nope, no dad, either." Lane cast his eyes downward again. "It's just me and my mom."

"That's different. You have no choice," James said.

Lane looked up, biting his lip. "I don't mind. It's my mom, you know."

"Orders up. Here you go, guys," the teenage crewman said as he pushed the baskets toward them. "Condiments are over there."

"Thanks." Lane followed the point. He grabbed a bottle of malt vinegar, another of catsup, and a handful of napkins. He nodded to the food, then to James, and said, "Take that to Kyle, will you?"

"No problem," James said, and he walked the treasure chest over to the booth, almost losing a chicken peg leg.

Lane watched the two tables interact and felt like an outsider. The insecurity was fleeting. He sat in an empty booth behind Kyle and Jenny, and the tall pleather seat back almost cut off the view of his friends. James scooted into the booth on the other side and stared. Lane ignored him as he shook a bottle of vinegar, letting it drizzle on top of the fried fish planks and soak some of the French fries beneath.

"You like that stuff?" James asked.

"What, you don't?" Lane ate a fry.

"Nah, that's too gross for me." James bit into a piece of fish, causing a little grease to drip down his chin.

"If you say so." Lane took a bite of his own fish, careful not to let it drip.

Wiping his mouth with a napkin, Lane looked over at Troy and Don, who were motioning and animated about their wave encounters. "How did you end up knowing Don?"

James chewed his mouthful carefully. "I met him at the pool last year. We hit it off and got high after his lifeguard shift one day, and it became a regular thing."

"You hung out with him and Tony?" Lane asked.

"Yeah, we hung out," James said, sipping his drink.

"What happened?" Lane's curiosity grew.

"Don hooked up with Melissa and got in with Troy's surfer crowd." James glanced across the dining room. "I kind of got squeezed out."

Lane pulled off another piece of battered cod with his plastic fork, waiting for James to continue.

"I can't surf." James shrugged and bit into a hush puppy.

Lane laughed. "That's cool. I can't surf either."

"Tony bailed and now hangs out with a rough crowd. You've seen him," James said.

Lane took another bite and said, "He's always asking me for a place to crash. I feel bad, but I try to avoid him."

Eyes growing big, James said, "Well, don't think I'm like that cat."

"Nope," Lane said, looking up and catching James's blue eyes. "I don't think you're like that at all."

"Cool," James said, their words lingering for a moment. His body language relaxed a little as he motioned to the booth behind him. "So, if Ted is Tammy's brother, how come she ain't here?"

"She had to go to church," Lane said with a sigh.

"What, all day?" James lowered his voice and asked, "What happened at the drive-in last night?"

Lane leaned in closer. "We talked and smoothed things over. It's cool."

James gave him a look. "I don't buy it, Lane," he said, picking up another hush puppy off of his plate.

"I swear we did." Lane swallowed and, reluctant, continued. "After she slapped me."

"Oh man," James said, chuckling. "That's such a hoot. You have such a way with women."

"No better than you. Anyway, she slapped me for what happened the last time. We talked it out, that's all," Lane said.

"The drive-in ain't for talking; it's for making out," James said, enjoying Lane's discomfort.

Lane felt flustered. "Tammy ain't here because she only wants to be friends."

"Friends, huh?" James smiled. "I guess you blew it with her." He sounded relieved.

"Yeah, but it's no big deal," Lane said.

"Look around," James said. "We're the odd men out."

"What are you talking about?" Lane felt nervous.

"Every guy is in a couple." James leaned in. "Except for us."

"We're going to the beach for Chrissakes," Lane said, trying to keep his voice down. "There'll be chicks everywhere."

"Right on. I was just pointing out the obvious." James leaned back into the booth.

Lane was about to say something more when Sally popped up behind James, peering over the top of the seat.

Lane changed his tune. "What's going on, Sally?"

"Nothing." Sally pushed her glasses back up. "You know, your friend is really cute."

"I'm sure he knows," Lane said, looking from her back to James, who subtly shook his head.

"Uh, um, thanks." James craned his neck and whispered, "Aren't you on a date?"

"Maybe." Sally winked. "I just wanted you to know."

James was smiling, but his cheeks were flushed. "I think you're a stone fox."

"Really?" Sally appraised him. "I don't know if I believe you."

"Nah, I mean it." James faltered. "If...if you weren't with some-one...that is."

Lane recognized the behavior in himself, the fear of being pressured to go all the way with a girl, and wondered about James.

Rolling her eyes, Sally slid down with a "Bye, boys."

"Dammit, I thought she was with Ted," James whispered.

"Maybe he's just babysitting her?" Lane enjoyed the reversal.

"I hope that's not true," James said, flashing a glance at Lane, gauging him.

Sizing his new friend up, Lane asked, "How come you don't have a girl, James?"

James seemed taken aback, flustered at the brashness of the question. "I don't know. I, uh, I just haven't... you know... met anyone I like... yet." James brushed the bangs off his forehead. "Maybe I'm not interested right now."

"That makes two of us." He was a little breathless, there was an energy between them he'd not felt before. He'd dreamed about leaving with Kyle, but that was never real, never possible. He continued, "I want to get out of the Heights before it's too late."

"Right on." James nodded. "Now's the time, man."

Lane added, "No, really, as soon as my mom gets better, I want to hit the road."

"That would be a trip." James bit his finger and said, "I want out of here too."

"Let's make it happen before the summer ends. We can hitch to California and start over," Lane said, dreamy and staring into the distance, into some future he could only imagine.

"Hitchhike? No way. I've got a bike we can ride." James looked Lane over. His voice lowered. "I like you. You're different."

"Different from what?" Lane's eyes widened. Fear struck him. Excitement, too.

"I don't know. Just different. Like me," James said.

Like me. The words echoed and the boys stared at each other in silence.

A commotion broke the moment between them, and they looked to the side to see the gang getting up to leave.

Kyle came up to their table with Jenny by his side and said, "Eat up. It's time to fly."

"Give me a sec." Lane stuffed his mouth with fries, chewing madly.

"We'll meet you outside." James wolfed down the rest of his fish, making a mess.

Troy and Don laughed at a private joke on the way out, while Angie and Melissa stayed close behind, immersed in some dramatic conversation of their own. Sally winked at James, who choked for a moment. Lane laughed and almost spat out what he was chewing. His mirth died when he saw Ted, who was staring at him like he wanted to maim him. Don pulled the rope, ringing the bell at the front of the shop, and the tension broke. Jenny went for the door, Kyle made a detour to the restroom, and Don lagged behind as the others made it outside to the parking lot to the sound of the fading bell.

"Hurry up, man." Lane urged James to chew.

"I am," James mumbled, eating the rest of his food on the way to the trash can.

Lane tossed his unfinished portion in the can and moved aside for James to do his business. Looking back, he saw Kyle and Don standing by the restroom door. They made a stealthy exchange and pocketed something unseen. James nudged Lane to move on.

Outside, the sun was heating the day in full force. Don ran out and picked Melissa up, spinning her around. Troy gave Angie a kiss. The surfing gang loaded up—the girls were practically on the guys' laps—in the cab of Troy's bright yellow '69 Chevy truck. Two long surfboards, waxed and strapped down, lay in its bed. Next to them, Ted opened the door for Sally to get in his candy-apple red '71 Volkswagen Super Beetle with its curved windshield and slightly longer body than the regular VW Bug. And taking her time, Jenny leaned on the hood of Kyle's super-blue '70 Challenger. The dreamy, faraway look of love shone in her eyes. Kyle walked with a strut down the wooden gangway, basking in her attention as he came around.

James nudged Lane again. "Let's go look at that car, man."

"Dammit, James, I don't want to go messing around." Lane smiled, despite himself.

"Come on, real quick," James said, tugging Lane's shirt and winking.

The strange danger of the situation secretly excited Lane, so he followed James. As they neared the left-behind El Camino, the signs of abandonment were clear. Pollen lay thick over the windows, obscuring the view of the interior.

James touched the glass, leaving a fingerprint smudge on the side window. He rubbed together his middle and index fingers to clean them, then wiped them off on his pants leg.

Through the streak, Lane saw school books and a pack lying on the passenger seat. "This is creepy, man."

"It sure is," James whispered, savoring the intensity of the moment.

"Look in the bed." Lane pointed to a shiny object. "There's something in there."

James used a finger to dig it out of the dirt in a groove of the El Camino bed. "It's a weird key."

Lane took it from James's hand and felt a chill on the back of his neck. "That's no ordinary key, man. It's a handcuff key."

"Whoa, that's sick." James took it back. "Wait, how do you know that?"

A loud metallic thud rang out, causing both Lane and James to jump. James almost dropped the key but closed his warm hand over it.

Kyle hit the hood of his car with the palm of his hand again for emphasis. "Jump in the back! We're outta here!"

Lane took a last look at the forlorn car and the closed dumpster beside it. James caught Lane's thought and laughed a little at the ridiculousness of it all.

Troy signed them two fingers for peace and peeled out to the girls' excited screams. The Super Beetle with Ted and Sally inside crawled out of the parking lot, left behind in a cloud of dust from the Chevy truck's spinning tires.

Jenny gave a kind smile and turned up the radio with "I'm Free" by The Who setting the mood. James jumped in the back and scooted over. Lane just had time to shut the door as Kyle took off to catch up to their friends, who were farther down Yale Street. The music cleared Lane's mind of any troubling thoughts. Jenny sang along with the lyrics, and Kyle drummed his fingers on the steering wheel as they left the Heights. James seemed to relax even more, leaving his unspoken home problems further behind.

Revving the engine into a roar of power, Kyle passed Troy and cut up to Interstate 10. Troy pushed his Chevy, but it was no match for the Dodge. The chase was on, and they barreled down the highway to the I-45 exit. Downshifting, they slowed at the ramp just in case the cops were out.

Twelve

The scree-scree noise grated the silence of the house in its repetition as the metal scouring pad wiped back and forth, cleaning the knife. Blood and soap suds swirled down the kitchen drain. The teenager's glasses fogged from the steam, and he wiped them absently on his sleeve as sweat dripped into the water flow from his long, stringy hair. The clean knife dropped with a clang into the metal toolbox on the tile counter. He picked up the last bloody implement. Hair and gore stuck to its serrated blade.

Behind him, another man whistled as he walked down the hallway. He looked inside the backroom and found it to his satisfaction with a freshly mopped floor, drying in the summer heat. Even the board was clean, although its presence seemed ominous near the mattress on the floor. He paced the room, stopping in the corner. There was hint of fire in his eyes—not as bright as the night before—as he picked up a bloody blue paisley bandana. He caught his reflection in the standing mirror, the one he liked to watch his victims with, and smiled.

The image was of an ordinary man going to work, wearing his HL&P uniform to check transformers in neighborhood backyards and visit family homes to fix their electricity. No one would expect this man to be a monster.

The man carried the bandana to the garage, careful not to get his hand bloody. In the dark space, he dropped it on top of a cage, eliciting a whimper from within. No reaction. No remorse. He shut the inner door and went out the back, not acknowledging his teenage accomplice at the sink.

In the driveway, he got into his work vehicle, a dirty white '65 Ford Econoline Van. Backing out, he was careful to avoid the dark red '68 Plymouth GTX parked on the curb. He felt good for the day, but he knew it would not last. It never did. The urge was getting stronger.

The man thought of the teenage boy he saw in the Heights and breathed in. He knew his name now and tested it on his lips. "Lane Bowden, maybe you'll be the one."

Thirteen

The Houston cityscape passed by on the left as the orange Gulf Oil sign turned on top of a tiered, 1920s Art Deco skyscraper. Downtown formed out of a mix of ornate buildings and smoother modern high-rises surrounded by a ribbon of freeway on all sides. The Challenger traveled part of that ribbon on the elevated portion of I-45, about a third of the way up, which gave an immaculate view of the passing buildings.

The radio newsbreak cut in: "The Watergate scandal is intensifying as John Dean's testimony has put heat on Nixon with calls for his resignation. Troops continue to withdraw from Vietnam, but the bombings in Cambodia continue, fueling anti-war protests for peace. Now that the draft is over, there is a call for the Runaway Youth Act since one in ten youth run away. Missing person reports are up, but it's no crime to split, so call home if you are out there on the road. Expect sunny skies today and a high around 90 degrees. Now back to the jam with Pink Floyd on Rock 101 KLOL."

The cha-ching of cash registers opened up the song, "Money."

"Runaways, what a trip." Lane thought about what it would be like on the road.

"I can't believe there are so many," James said.

"Hell, they're the lucky ones. I wish they would play some Zeppelin on the radio. That show at the Coliseum was beyond cool," Kyle said, stealing glances at the fleeting view of the concert hall's boxy structure, next to city hall, as he drove.

"You lucky bastard, I really wanted to go to that show." James sighed, absorbed in the mostly deserted city.

Lane looked at Jenny, who pulled her legs up onto the seat. He followed her gaze to watch Kyle drive, then moved his own gaze back to James, whose mind was clearly somewhere else. Remembering to look, he turned the opposite way and saw St. Joseph's Hospital, where he was born. The sight pulled a faint melancholy over him, but the blinding sun burned it away as the sweet incense of lit grass filled the enclosed space of the car.

Kyle passed the joint to Jenny, who took it between her delicate, manicured fingers. She lightly toked and coughed, causing Kyle to laugh. Sunlight shone through the windshield from passing clouds, creating a soft and sharp alternating light. Pink Floyd eased into "Wish You Were Here."

Lane smoked his turn and thought, *These are my favorite moments. Everything's cool. Feeling the warm light, riding in this muscle car, and seeing my friends are absolute perfection. Wow, I'm definitely stoned.*

Enjoying the relaxation that washed over him, he toked some more before passing it to James. "Take it."

"That's what I'm talking about," James said, back in the moment.

The Challenger passed by Gulfgate Mall. Lane could see the tiny figures of a family walking over a caged footbridge as they crossed over the 610 Loop intersection, from the mall to the movie theater on the other side. A strange carnival-like motel, The Carousel, grabbed his attention for a moment with its frozen carousel on a rusted pole. Lane's mind drifted as the road went on.

"Just up here is Hobby Airport." Kyle pointed it out.

Everyone looked out on the right, but there was nothing except a narrow strip of water, fields, and some industrial-looking warehouses.

"Back in there, behind that bayou?" James asked dubious and high.

"No, silly, the airport is farther up, by Telephone Road." Jenny rubbed her legs, satisfied that they were smooth.

"I've never hung out there. I've only been by it." Lane felt content for a change.

"There's a cool spot right behind the runway where you can park and watch the planes land and take off at night." Kyle's face lit up.

"I would love to see that. I bet it's beautiful." Jenny gently rocked back and forth, curled up like an obtuse ball.

"I'll show you sometime, babe." Kyle passed the joint to Jenny, but she shook her head, so it went to Lane.

"I bet he will," James murmured.

Lane elbowed James, passing the joint to complete the circle. "Here you go."

James took it, eager. "This is some far-out grass."

"Yep, it makes the drive peaceful." Kyle took the roach and ground it out in the ashtray.

"This is great." Lane motioned around the car. "This trip and all of you."

Jenny giggled. "I like you when you're high."

"I like you too...when I'm high," Lane said, feeling goofy.

"Good to know." Kyle gave Lane a warning look in the rearview mirror.

James leaned back, blowing thin smoke out of his nose. He smiled and closed his eyes. "I could take a nap."

"Me too," Lane said, letting himself drift.

The Rock 101 KLOL DJ's soothing, radio voice came through the speakers: "This is Crash in your dash, chilling out with Floyd on a Sunday—three in a row—now going to 'The Dark Side of the Moon.'"

The landscape changed around the Challenger, becoming more barren and marshy as the car tore down the highway toward the Gulf of Mexico.

WAVES CRASHED ALONG AN *infinite shore; water stretched to the horizon, disturbed and uneasy. Lane looked into the distance. There was not a cloud in the sky, yet the sun seemed far away and cold. Nothing stirred in the sea or air, save his mother standing in the crashing surf, holding a younger version of him in her arms. Wearing a green, one-piece bathing suit, her freckles showed on her pale skin while her mane of brown hair blew about. Lane could not see the face of his younger self. It was a blur.*

The water broke around them, almost engulfing them in its embrace. She looked at Lane and smiled, and the past flooded back across the years. Memories of growing up—the flash of better times, even happiness—poured over him as the ocean poured over her. And with the last wave, she vanished, taking a part of him to the other side.

Lane stared at the calm, tranquil sea from the shoreline, feeling the cold sand between his toes and the unfathomable loss of innocence.

Fourteen

A LOUD CRY FROM a seagull startled Lane, and he opened his eyes to discover James asleep on his shoulder. Reclined in the backseat, Lane stayed still as he watched the coastline with peaceful awe. The sea wind blew his bangs back and forth. Over the low rumble of the Challenger, he heard another bird cry. The causeway bridge was high, with a panoramic view of the bay and Galveston Island. With the radio off and the windows down, the sounds of the approaching destination filled the car, and the smell of salt and ocean life wafted through its interior.

Lane dared not move. He was uncomfortable yet excited at how close James was. He kept one eye open to watch the scenery. Palm trees punctuated the welcome sign at the end of the causeway, bringing feelings of sun and sand as the freeway ended and became Broadway Boulevard. Tall oleander bushes in full yellow and pink blooms marked the way to the beach, growing erratic in its median.

The warmth was nice. Lane felt James's breath on his neck and tried to ignore it as the world passed by.

Swaths of sprawled-out cemeteries lined the boulevard, interspersed among the run-down mansions and small convenience stores and shops. Markers, tombs, and grand mausoleums—mostly relative to the epic hurricane of 1900 that destroyed Galveston—teased the eye.

Why are the bodies so close to the road? The thought unsettled Lane. He shifted in the back seat and stretched.

James stirred, lifted his head up from Lane's shoulder, and looked up, sleepy. "Oh, sorry for drooling on you, man."

"It's cool." Lane watched as James wiped his chin and sat up straight.

They shared an uncertain look, and Lane was glad no eyes were watching them in the rearview mirror. *Why does he make me so nervous?*

Jenny pressed the radio buttons to Kyle's chagrin and said, "I want to hear something fun."

Kyle rolled his eyes, but let her have her way. Jenny pressed again and again until she found a channel to her liking.

A smooth radio voice announced, "Here is one out of the bottom of the pile, The Beach Boys with 'Sail on Sailor' on calm, KAUM 96.5 FM."

Kyle watched Jenny wiggle and did not say a word through the pained look on his face. He hit the brakes at a stop light. The motion jolted Lane and James into the backseat's vinyl cushion.

A looming aqua bronze statue of Lady Victory holding out a laurel crown blocked the sun. Roman columns were at her base, where her sisters, Defiance and Peace, sat in judgment of a past battlefield. The heroes and lost soldiers of the Texas War of Independence made up the rest of the milieu.

"That statue freaks me out." Lane pointed and James's eyes followed.

"Everything seems to freak you out." James laughed, but he felt the power of the sculpture and lost his edge. "It's weird. What do you think it means?"

"I don't know. Maybe it's something about finding peace after the war. Maybe..." Lane lost his train of thought as he stared at it.

The light changed. Closer to the end of the road, the sound of crashing surf intensified in force as they cruised to the last light before the coast.

"Hey, look, there's the ocean." James leaned forward for a better view.

"It's the seawall. Look down there!" Lane pointed at it as the car rolled to a stop. "Dammit, we're not far enough up."

James looked at the seawall, then back to Lane. "What's down that way?"

"There's a hotel called The Flagship. It has these big, topless mermaids carved in stone on the front. I always wanted to stay there because it's right over the water," Lane said, full of disappointment.

"On a pier?" James asked.

Lane smiled. "Yeah, imagine what it'd be like to have the waves under you while you sleep."

"It'd be fantastic." James looked dreamy at the thought.

"One day. When I have some money." Lane sighed and slumped a little.

"You and me both." James took a deep breath of sea air.

The bright yellow '69 Chevy stopped hard at the light, and the surfboards shifted in the back of the truck. The girls inside laughed, and Don flashed a peace sign while Troy idled the rest of the way up beside the Challenger, yelling something lost to the music. Without thinking, Kyle turned the radio down, and Jenny gave him a frustrated look for his action.

"I said, let's race to the gate when the light changes!" Troy yelled again.

Kyle scanned the road and saw that the coast was clear. "Alright, but you're gonna lose, buddy."

"Hey, I got to try, man." Troy grinned, his sun-bleached hair whipping across his glassy eyes.

Jenny turned the music back up and returned to her groove. Lane and James sat back, ready for takeoff. James's hand slipped, grazed across to Lane's knee, and lingered for a second. Lane felt eyes on him. The hand slipped away and neither acknowledged the moment.

Gripping the wheel as Troy revved the Chevy's engine, Kyle changed the radio back to KLOL. Led Zeppelin's "The Ocean" filled the air, causing him to grin sublimely as the light changed green.

The cars tore off, racing to full speed, leaving the traffic behind. Kyle jammed and shifted gears, crossing the Challenger over to the wrong side of the roadway. The beach road was a paved, two-lane affair, one that curved and winded through the dunes to the entrance of East Beach.

The Challenger hummed like a finely tuned beast as the odometer edged past sixty to eighty in mere seconds. Troy's Chevy truck kept pace, pulling out some horsepower from its 350 engine. Screams came from both vehicles as the race twisted along the sandy track. Kyle punched it and edged ahead, passing Troy. Lane laughed and saw the same wide grin on James's face as they shared the rush.

"Oh, shit!" Kyle exclaimed as he downshifted and braked, coasting back and pulling behind the Chevy.

Troy slowed down, too, at the sight of a black and white '72 Dodge Polara police cruiser that sat in wait beside a dune. A 'good ol' boy' sheriff with a cowboy hat and dark sunglasses was behind the wheel.

Braking hard, Kyle managed not to lock the tires up. Directly in front, Troy swerved a little as he slowed. Kyle's reflexes were fast, almost like second nature, and he avoided a collision. The cars continued to slow, but as soon as they passed, the police car's flashing red lights lit up.

Kyle gritted his teeth, waiting for the bad news. Jenny put her feet on the floor for the first time during the ride, clenching her jaw and looking over her shoulder out the rear window at the cop car gaining on them. Lane's face dropped, and he gave James a desperate look as the radio rocked on without an audience.

The police cruiser came up behind them, sirens blaring. With an offsetting suddenness, it turned around in a cloud of sand, speeding off the opposite way.

"Oh my god, I almost had a heart attack." Jenny pulled her legs back up into a more comfortable position.

"You and me both, babe." Kyle loosened his grip on the wheel. "Damn, I need a beer."

Breathing out in a steady sigh, Lane said, "I think I lost my high."

James, with wide eyes, turned and exhaled sharply. "You guys are crazy, but damn, it's fun!"

"Fun?" Jenny turned on James. "Are you kidding me?"

"Yeah, it is!" Lane laughed, breaking the tension.

"Right on." James laughed with him and they shared a palm grip with a twist.

Jenny rolled her eyes. "You two are not right."

Ignoring them, Kyle said, "I just can't wait to park and walk this off." He looked in the rearview mirror, just in case the police were coming back with reinforcements.

Kyle drove through the overarching entrance with the sun glinting off the Challenger's super-blue hood. Lane and James looked out the back window, and the police cruiser was nowhere in sight. Jenny casually grabbed Kyle's arm as a faded, hand-painted sign that read, "Apffel Park—East Beach" came into view.

A beach girl in a tan, tight bikini took the entrance fee from inside a wooden booth.

Lane sat straight. "That's odd. There usually is a wait to get in."

The beach girl reached down, finishing the transaction with a weak smile. The distinct smell of Coppertone suntan lotion wafted into the car.

"Maybe it's almost full." Kyle felt unsettled as he took his change.

"Look, there're lots of people here." James nodded out the window.

"There are." Lane leaned back. Pushing away his anxiety, he glanced at James and the surf beyond him.

Kyle drove forward, kicking up soft sand under the tires. "It'll be cooler when we park."

Sticking her head out the window, soaking in some sun, Jenny said, "Feel the heat. It's so nice."

Kyle turned the wheel, and his lip curled up in a lopsided grin at the view. "It really is nice."

A couple of small wooden signs marked the way as the tires hit the soft-packed sand, spelling out guidelines for "No Glass Containers" and "Beware of Undertow".

They passed rows upon rows of lined-up cars and trucks in both directions. A slow stream of cruisers made their way from one side to the other, leaving ruts in the sand. Radios competed with ocean noise.

Troy pulled into a spot. Before the truck stopped, Melissa, Don, and Angie jumped out of its cab, looking frazzled.

Kyle pulled in and said, "Damn, that was close. My hands are shaking a little."

Jenny gave Kyle a quick kiss on the lips and opened her door. "Oh, I'm so glad to be out of the car."

Ted parked next to them, his VW Beetle chugging along to a stop.

"Hey Sally, you won't believe what happened," Jenny said, walking over to gossip.

Kyle hit the seat lever, shrugged at Lane, and followed Jenny to the others.

Lane crawled out of the back seat. The softness of the sand felt good, even with his boots on. He turned and wobbled, bumping into James. "My heart is still racing from that scene."

"Hell, I almost pissed my pants." James looked around, searching for something. "I've kind of got to pee now."

"The head is way back over there, man," Lane said, pointing towards a gazebo of sorts with concessions and outdoor showers.

"Damn, that's far." James eyed the new group that Kyle and the gang were greeting and asked, "Who are the chicks?"

Lane squinted at the foursome of beach bunnies, putting towels and sunscreen back into a mustard-colored '71 Chevy Impala with a white top. He pointed out the ones he knew and said, "The tall one leaning in the car is Dawn, and Iris is the skinny brunette talking to her."

"What about the tan one?" James pointed. "Next to the big girl."

Lane shrugged. "I don't know."

James watched the girls finish packing up. "It looks like they're getting ready to go."

"It sure does." Lane nodded toward some jocks and a two-tone pickup. "That is why Kyle looks pissed off over there."

"I thought he always looked like that," James joked.

"He does." Lane smirked, then asked, "What kind of truck is that?"

"It looks like a Jeep—one of the new ones, I think." James looked around, popping his jaw. He saw someone he knew and quickly looked away.

"What's up, man?" Lane asked James.

James tittered and opened and closed his mouth.

Before he could get an answer, Lane saw what made James turn: two long-haired guys trying to stow two small Styrofoam ice chests in the trunk of an orange and black top '69 Pontiac GTO. The rope handle of one chest caught on the trunk latch, spilling beer and ice everywhere.

"Are those Tony's friends?" Lane asked.

"Yeah." James looked at the ground, kicking at something absently. "The one with the beard is Maurice, and the other is Brother John."

"John a monk or something?" Lane looked perplexed.

"No, they call him Brother John because he passes out acid like communion and promises that you will see Jesus if you drop it," James said.

"Oh," Lane managed, not knowing whether to laugh or let it go.

James's eyes widened like saucers. "The pigs are shaking people down."

A group of sheriff deputies appeared behind Maurice and Brother John. A heated interrogation formed.

"Oh no," Lane blurted out as he watched Tony shamble up and spill some desperate tale to their friends.

"What?" James fidgeted with his legs.

"There's Tony, and that always means trouble," Lane said with a sigh.

"Dammit, I really gotta pee, man," James said, shifting back and forth. He found no solace in the faraway restrooms, with long lines streaming past rainbow umbrellas.

"Don't go. Bad things are going down." Lane watched as one of the Galveston County deputies slammed Maurice against the GTO and searched him.

"Nah, I ain't going nowhere, but it's time for all of us to split." James checked the pills in his pocket.

The beach bunnies quietly drove away. Ted and Sally tried to follow suit, jumping inside the VW Beetle, but it was a long moment as they waited for their car to backfire into life.

Jenny hurried back to the gang and whispered, "We've got to go. They're busting anyone with long hair."

"Yeah, it looks messed up here," James said, watching the vibe change.

"Let's get Kyle and split," Lane said.

Ted motioned with his head to leave, and he turned around and yelled, "Get in your cars and go!"

"We're going, man!" Lane yelled back.

Sally stuck her head out of the VW Beetle window. "See you at the ferry, Jenny."

"Be careful. We'll be there soon." Jenny looked at the mounting police presence with unease.

Across the sand, a sheriff stepped in, taking off his sunglasses, to assess the situation.

"Hey, watch the car, man!" Brother John complained. The words echoed on the beach, while a deputy roughly searched his pockets.

"Come on." Lane nudged James.

Lane and James walked into the mild hysteria of the gang, and Jenny followed in a daze. Silent and wide-eyed, they watched an argument unfold.

"I can't go with them." Tony looked from Kyle to Troy for some help. "I'm holding."

"I ain't responsible for you, Tony," Kyle warned.

"I don't know what to do. They busted my ride," Tony said.

"Let's just get out of here before we get into trouble." Melissa pulled at Don's shirt. "Come with me to the truck."

"Troy, let's go," Don said, allowing his girl to pull him away.

"We've got to go now." Troy made up his mind but did not feel right about the situation. "Let's meet at High Island."

"Don't leave him with me." Kyle bowed up.

"Fine, Tony, you can ride in the back," Troy offered, avoiding Angie's eyes as she stormed off.

"Baby, I'm scared." Jenny snuggled close to Kyle's side.

"Don't worry." Kyle consoled Jenny and then conceded to Troy. "Alright, I'll see you on the ferry."

"Be cool, man," Troy said, slapping hands with Kyle.

Kyle looked at the spreading chaos on the beach. "Let's roll out of this place."

Lane half-jogged behind them and said, "This is nuts."

"Total pig convention, man," James mumbled, matching Lane's speed.

Kyle opened the door to the Challenger, and Jenny got in, holding the seat up. He went around to the driver's side, wearily watching the surroundings.

"You can't go anywhere anymore," Lane said, crawling in the back and scooting over to make room for James.

As James maneuvered his body behind the seat, Lane got a whiff of his natural scent and swallowed. "Except for the Heights," James said, still watching the cops.

Lane checked out the chaos, then James, and added, "That's one cool thing about the neighborhood," with a nervous laugh.

"There might be another." James stared at him, then moved his legs as the seat came back.

Not sure of what to say, Lane shifted his feet in the tight space.

Kyle shut his door as soon as Lane and James settled in. Jenny placed her feet firmly on the floorboard while Kyle reached under the seat and stashed his bag in his pants, feeling like an outlaw.

The Challenger's engine rumbled to life, and its noise over-came any chance of a quiet getaway. The sheriff stared with the cold eye of the law. Kyle moved along, hoping the long arm would not follow.

"Everyone, be cool," Kyle whispered in the dead air.

The radio was silent for the seemingly endless beach cruise. One of the black-and-white Dodge Polara patrol cars turned to follow them. There were no flashers on, yet a sense of dread filled the car.

Lane looked at James, slightly turning his head. He saw a sher-iff and a deputy, but their dark sunglasses blocked their expres-sions. In turn, James swallowed and looked ahead. Jenny turned to the side, then back to Kyle, her hair blowing in the breeze.

Reaching into his pants, Kyle slipped out a handful of grass, making sure to keep it low. Out of sight. "Here, pass this back."

"What are you doing?" Jenny trembled.

"We've got to eat it. There's no way those rednecks are catching me," Kyle said.

"Just shove it into the seat," Lane begged.

"Everyone is going to eat it and act naturally for Chrissakes," Kyle ordered, angrily looking the gang over.

"Oh, Kyle, I can't." Jenny shook her head but took a handful of grass.

"Give me some," James said, sticking his hand over the console. "You take some too, Lane."

Lane obeyed and watched his friends chew on the grass like mad cows. It would have been funny if his heart wasn't beating so fast from the adrenaline and fear.

The gate was close, but the cruiser was closer. Kyle reached for some more grass and stopped. Behind them, the cops took off, swinging the cruiser around back to the beach.

"I can't believe it. We made it!" Kyle finished some silent prayers and swallowed his comeuppance for breaking the law.

Jenny spat out the window as they crossed over to Ferry Road. "I'm never going back to that beach again."

"You know, this is kind of tasty." James was still chewing.

Lane made obvious and exaggerated chewing motions, showing his teeth. "It's delicious."

Kyle wiped his mouth and drove down the mercifully empty road. "Check it out; the ferry is boarding. Perfect!"

Jenny spat again and scraped at her tongue with her long nails. "I need to rinse my mouth out."

James looked mischievously at Lane, who beat him to the punch. "Don't say it."

Shrugging, James kept chewing. "Can you get high this way?"

"Sure, haven't you ever had brownies?" Lane licked some of the green mulch off his front teeth.

"It just takes longer to hit you." Kyle smacked on a mouthful of green.

Jenny spat a third time. "I hope so, because I need to chill out after that affair."

"We'll stay late and build a fire." Kyle smiled, looking like a kid eating candy.

"Yeah, man. That's an ace idea." James tried to swallow. "Damn, this is hard to chew."

"Take your time and savor it." Lane chortled, sending a spray of grass spittle onto James's arm.

"What the hell, man? You spit on me." Looking offended, James wiped his arm.

"Sorry, James. I'm blowing my cool." Lane cracked up, spraying again.

"Hey, hey, hey... No more!" James choked, sending green drool out of the corner of his mouth.

"Oh man, that's not right. You look like a bog monster from *Scooby Doo*," Lane said, choking up too.

James growled like a beast, causing both of them to bust up.

"Cut it out back there. I've had enough trouble for the day." Kyle got serious.

Jenny shook her head, hiccupped, and started laughing for no particular reason.

"Maybe it doesn't take that long." Kyle lost his melodramatic frown and busted up laughing.

Lane couldn't catch his breath, thrilled that James was in the same state of mind.

Fifteen

The view through the bars of the cage seemed dull and muted. Faint light seeped in from a crack too far away to do any good. Naked, the sandy blond runaway tested the lock for the hundredth time. The connected chain rattled on the metal. He had seen what had happened to other boys and could not believe he had survived so long.

The inner door to the garage opened, and a yellow-hued light clicked on, illuminating the darkness from a single bulb.

A scruffy teenager walked to the cage, peering inside. "You got yourself in a fine mess, Billy."

Billy twisted on his haunches inside the tight space. "Look, I know I can fix this."

"You know what I had to promise *him* to get you off that board?" He leaned in closer, eyeing him like a trapped animal.

"Whatever it is, I'll do it." Billy shifted, running a hand down a crusty cut on his bare side.

The scruffy teenager tilted his head. "Anything?"

"Yeah, man." Billy's eyes were haunted and wide. "Just let me out of here."

The scruffy teenager hesitated, then the lock clicked, and the chain fell loose to the concrete floor.

Billy trembled as he shambled out of the cage in a squat. He felt vulnerable but steadied himself and rose, feeling the sensation return to his numb legs. Glancing at his blood-streaked crotch, he hoped he wasn't too messed up.

"Tony is a problem. He knows too much." The scruffy teenager threw him some torn jeans.

"I can handle him." Billy met the other's stare head-on, putting a leg in his jeans by feel.

"There's a bigger thing. It's someone *he* wants." He eyed the dried blood.

"Who's that?" Billy carefully slid into the other leg. He put a hand out for balance and bloodied his fingers on a blue bandana.

"It's a guy named Lane Bowden who lives in the Heights and sometimes hangs at the Bohemian Pool Hall. I want you to find him," he said, handing over the rest of Billy's clothes.

Billy slid on a dirty white muscle shirt, and his wound spotted the material. "And if he's with somebody?"

"No more than one other, and make sure they're fucked up." The scruffy teenager's lip curled.

"I'm done after this. You'll never see me again." Billy fought back panic, remembering being tied to the board and the man having his fun and shoving the glass rod inside him. The dull ache throbbed below.

"Yeah, sure. As long as you deliver." The scruffy teenager seemed sincere. "Find him and tell him you can score. You know where we hang out over there, at Graham Park."

"I can do that." Billy ran a hand through his hair.

"You're lucky. It could've been worse, like the bandana boy." He motioned to a body wrapped in plastic in the darkened corner.

"Nah, I got this." Billy swallowed and slipped his shoes on.

"Alright then." The scruffy teenager kicked the cage, and Billy flinched. "I'll drop you off in the Heights, then I've gotta get back for the night surf."

Billy knew better than to ask why they would go to the beach at night. Determined not to go back on the board or in the cage, he followed the scruffy teenager out of the dark garage. He would do whatever he had to do, even if someone else took his place.

Sixteen

The Bolivar Ferry crossed the bay from Galveston Island to a remote part of the Bolivar Peninsula. It was the only direct way there.

Kyle drove the Challenger right up the ramp onto the ferry, almost being the final vehicle aboard until a black '68 Buick Riviera boxed him in line. Rough sailors pulled up the gate, detached the ramp, and put blocks of wood under the tires of the vehicles on the edge of the ferry. Made of a few thick chains, the gate left the idea of a car sliding off into the depths of the bay apparent.

Kyle stepped out, leaving space for the backseat to empty out. On the opposite side, Jenny stretched, and she cowered when a seagull swooped too close.

"I hate birds! They freak me out," she said, swatting at the air.

James tried to ignore the strong taste of pot in his mouth and asked, "What did they ever do to you?"

"There was one in my backyard, and it used to wait and attack me every time I went outside," Jenny said. "I swear it had it out for me."

Lane, halfway paying attention, said, "It was probably just protecting its nest."

"No, they're plotting. Look at them. See how they call to each other," Jenny insisted. "It's like they know I'm here." She visibly shuddered.

James flinched as another gull swooped down. "Maybe she's right."

Lane nodded, more interested in the bay.

"Maybe y'all are high." Kyle jingled the car keys between his fingers while Jenny stared at the birds.

The ferry horn blew loudly, its deep sound vibrating the steel and concrete structure and jostling the gang. Lane felt the sea breeze with James close at his side as he checked out the swirling motion of the churning water.

On shore, at the landing, the sheriff stepped out of his Dodge Polara cruiser and watched the ferry depart behind silver reflective sunglasses.

Lane looked up, noticing the staring lawman. "Hey, Kyle, that sheriff is checking us out."

"That's it." Kyle lowered his voice and said, "We're staying down at High Island late until all of this mess blows over."

The stiff, broad-shouldered sheriff leaned forward, legs unmoving on the side of his cruiser, his hand casually resting near his gun. Sunglasses covered his eyes, yet the feel of his stare was strong as the ferry moved away, crossing the water.

"Screw him." James looked at Kyle, gauging his reaction, and said, "Anyway, it would take him a long time to come after us."

"True, but my nerves feel shot." Kyle breathed out, trying to relax.

"I'm thirsty." Jenny sidled up to Kyle, rubbing his chest with a manicured hand.

"Get us a beer, Kyle." Lane stared at the sheriff, who farther away seemed less defined.

Kyle put the key in the trunk lock and popped it open. Inside, he unlatched one of the ice chests and passed out a round of Lone Star. "Be cool and keep them low, out of sight."

The gang pulled the tabs off together, and they all drank a gulp of the refreshing brew.

"Save the rings for me. I want to make a necklace later." Jenny held out a palm, and metal tabs filled it.

"Where's the head in this place?" James looked up at the second deck for solace.

"I'll show you. I've got to go too." Lane motioned for James to follow. Holding his beer close to his waist, he weaved around the bumpers of the close-parked cars.

"Wait for me." James caught up.

Lane asked, "Have you been on this ferry before?" as they climbed a set of narrow steps.

"Nah, man. I've only been to the beach a few times. Hell, I hardly have been out of the Heights," James admitted, listening to his voice echo in the stairway along with the clunks of footsteps.

Lined with windows and benches, the viewing level was humid. A few older couples and families rested or minded their unruly kids. Most of the other passengers were on the outside deck, along the rails that surrounded them, watching the water. The level's walls and floors were a joyless gray. In several spots, the paint had peeled back, revealing a darker shade. Lane and James found the restrooms in the middle; past them, another set of steps led to the helm.

Inside, the men's restroom felt confined and industrial, without a lot of space. Lane stood at the stainless steel urinal. He felt unbalanced by the movement of the boat. A metallic ring rang out as James urinated next to him, and he snuck a quick look.

"Oh my god, that's so much better," James said as he leaned a hand against the wall in relief.

"It sure is." Lane finally urinated, relieved that his shyness had not taken over as it did around some guys.

James zipped up and looked over as he picked up his beer off the back of the urinal. "Let's check out the deck."

Lane fumbled with his belt buckle but got it in place. Feeling weird at the moment, he said, "The view is fantastic. You'll dig it."

"I'm sure I will," James said, taking a swig.

Lane drank some of his beer, and the door banged open. An old man in a pleated plaid sports coat ambled in, and they slid past him out the door. Lane spilled a little beer on the back of his hand and licked it off without thinking. "I think I'm a little messed up, James."

"Me too, Lane." James looked around, and their eyes met for a moment.

The wind hit them hard as they stepped out of the enclosed viewing area. The smell of the sea, of the briny water, and of the living things swimming in it was strong. Gently pushing their way to the front, they found a spot on the rail with a clear view of water and, fairly far off, approaching land.

The warm air felt soothing on Lane's face as the ferry moved over the rough waters, away from trouble. He glanced at James. *It's cool to have made a new friend so fast.*

James caught his eye and asked, "What was it about the El Camino?"

The wind ruffled Lane's hair, and he remembered the connection. "I've seen it before."

"Where?" James moved closer to hear him.

"Over at Graham Park, and you won't believe this—Henley was there too," Lane said.

"No way." James paused. "Did you see Jamie?"

He shook his head and stared over the water. "I only saw Henley leaning into the car."

"He was probably just hooking him up with some dope." James shrugged. "What else could it be?"

"I don't know." Lane turned to James. "It just stuck with me, that's all."

"We should've looked in the dumpster, and we wouldn't be talking about this." James teased.

"Shut up," Lane said.

"I'm just saying." James ribbed him.

"I've seen this dark red '68 GTX hardtop at Henley's house and on the cruise last night. Lane added. "It kind of weirds me out." His words hung in the air, but James's attention was elsewhere now.

Looking in the green seawater, Lane saw movement. A fin broke the surface to descend, then rose again to skim the swells.

"Check it out!" Lane pointed down. "A dolphin!"

"Cool," James said, as he saw another dolphin join the first, swimming back and forth together near the bow. "How do they keep out of the boat's way?"

"I don't know. They're just fast." Lane beamed at the playful sight.

"They're so free, man." James watched a dolphin jump out of the sea and arc in a half-circle dive. Another dolphin followed, and they both disappeared into the ferry's wake.

"Aw, they're gone." Lane felt a little disappointed that the show was short.

James's attention moved to the people milling about the cars on the main deck. "So, who are the guys in the Jeep?"

"What guys?" Lane tried to focus on what James was talking about.

"Hey, snap out of it." James nudged him.

Lane blinked and muttered, "Sorry, man. I was still swimming with the dolphins."

"You're such a trip." James tasted his already warm beer and looked away from Lane's curious brown eyes. "Down there, in front of Troy's truck. Who are they?"

Lane looked down and saw Troy and Don animatedly talking with two jocks from Heights High. The taller jock looked up. Lane averted his gaze to the girls next to them, Angie and Melissa.

"Well?" James pressed.

"The tall one is Riley, and the other one is Conner. They're Bulldogs, Kyle's football buddies from before," Lane said quietly.

"What a joke." James sized them up. He showed no fear and did not look away when Riley met his gaze. "Guys like that always have something to prove."

The carload of beach bunnies entered the group, semi-circling the jocks.

Lane shook his head. "Maybe they're cool."

"Nah, they just want some dope, that's all. Mark my words; later on, one of them will start a fight." James looked Lane over. "Are you much of a fighter?"

"I can throw my own." Lane felt taken aback. "I just don't run in the same circles."

James said, "You can't avoid it. It's the way the world is. Especially if you're *different*."

"That may be true, but I don't care if it is." Lane pushed the stress away, ignoring the word different.

"It's cool. If there's trouble, there's two of us," James said, feeling confident.

"Yeah, you watch my back, and I'll watch yours." Lane felt his own confidence grow.

"We'll see." James saw Lane in a different light. "You want to get another beer?"

"Sure." Lane looked for the dolphins, but they had swum away or were just out of sight, hiding under the surface, like him.

"I dig this, man. It's really cool." James finished his can.

Lane chugged the rest of his beer and asked, "What?"

"I don't know. All of this." James gestured around.

"Just remember," Lane said, pointing to the metal-plated name of the boat, "we were on the R.S. Sterling."

"Alright?" James looked up at the sign, the sunlight, and the gulls competing for his attention. He tilted his head and asked, "What do you mean?"

"The time and the place, man. It's important to hang on to the cool things," Lane said, moving out of the way as a little girl pushed by his legs to get a look out through the railing.

"That's kind of heavy for a Heights kid." James gave Lane a playful shove.

"Let's grab another beer before we get to the landing," Lane said, feeling too serious. He hated getting stuck in his thoughts when he just wanted to hang out with James.

"Okay," James said, watching the land across the water. "Is that Bolivar?"

"Yeah, that was fast." Lane felt surprised to see how close the dock on the approaching shore was to the ferry, with a line of cars waiting and sailors bustling about.

The ferry horn rang out with a deep sound.

"Time sure flies by when you're high," James quipped.

"It sure does," Lane said, as he walked fast along the side, heading back the same way they came.

James followed. "Hey, slow down."

"Come on, we've got to hurry if we're going to have that beer," Lane said as he took off.

"Dammit, Lane. Wait up!" James ran after him, dodging passengers.

The horn sounded again. Lane took the stairs two at a time, jumping the last four to the bottom of the well. James copied his moves but tripped up on the last jump, and Lane saved him from going face-first into a wall.

"Whoa, thanks, man," James said, a little out of breath.

"You owe me," Lane said, with a curl of his lip.

"Oh yeah," James said, darting off between the cars back to the trunk of the Challenger.

Lane caught up to James at the car, and they got an eyeful of Kyle and Jenny making out in the front seat. He glanced at James, who shushed him with a finger to his lips as he quietly opened the trunk. James softly opened the tab of one beer can and offered a second. Lane opened the Lone Star and took a sip before losing his composure and giggling.

"Shut up, man," James snickered.

"Whether it's a car or a boat, I guess he's giving her a ride." Lane busted up, and foam poured out of the top of his beer.

"Yeah, I guess the train comes later," James said, chugging half his Lone Star.

"Why is that so funny?" Lane asked and swigged down some more beer.

"It just is," James said, choking on the last bit of foam.

Lane snorted, and beer came out of his nose. They both lost it.

"What the hell?" Kyle said, appearing out of nowhere. "You guys are so stupid." Kyle could not keep from laughing at them. "Get in the damn car."

"Alright, we're getting in." Lane tried to be serious, but his smile kept twitching back in place.

James said, "All aboard," and busted up again.

"I can't," Lane snickered through dribbling foam.

Kyle closed the trunk as the ferry horn sounded a third time. Inside the car, Jenny was red-faced but laughed at the sight of Lane and James, who fought to regain their composure. Kyle kissed Jenny, his eyes on the rearview mirror, daring them to say anything. Somehow, they maintained.

"Turn on the jam, baby," Jenny said.

"How far is it to High Island?" James switched gears.

"I think it's about thirty miles." Kyle clicked on the radio, moving the knob to clear the static.

"That's not far," James said, nodding his head to the soulful guitar-driven song "Over the Hills and Far Away" by Led Zeppelin.

"Yes, I love this album!" Kyle turned up the volume.

Jenny danced in her seat. "This is the new one, right?"

"Yeah, *Houses of the Holy*, it's Zen," Lane said, leaning back and taking it in.

James rocked in his seat. "Will you spark one up when we get off this boat?"

"Don't think I won't, little man." Kyle started the engine and followed the row of cars down the plank onto the dock.

The tires felt solid again on dry land. The Challenger left behind the cars chilling at the dock, passed the ones turning off at Fort

Travis for the battlements, and joined the rest to head down the peninsula on Highway 87.

Dunes drifted sand onto the road, lined with sturdy grass and low-lying brush of the mesquite and sage varieties. Nothing seemed to exist in abundance. Lane felt at peace with the warm, salty air blowing on his face and the deserted backdrop passing by the Challenger. With a lot of space in front and behind the car, the ride had a sense of openness.

A tall, black iron lighthouse came into view, dark and ominous—a strange omen. The music lightened the mood as pot smoke filled the car. Lane wondered about the history of the lighthouse: the dark, desperate nights, massive hurricanes, and the eerie peace of lighting the way in a dense fog. He watched his friends get high and realized he was too stoned to convey his thoughts.

SEVENTEEN

SOME ROADS NEVER END. Lane focused on the two-lane highway. The sight of water appeared on the left, occasionally on the right, and even for a brief stretch on both sides of the Challenger. The view was disorienting for Lane, and he was silently glad the car had slowed to turn off of the highway onto a secluded beach road.

Under the music, the hypnotic tone of the car's tires droned on. James was asleep, facing the opposite direction. In front, Jenny lay back, holding Kyle's hand while he drove the distance. Zeppelin tapered out, and the soothing radio voice of DJ Crash led to a set of Aerosmith. "Dream On" synced with the end of the road trip, giving it an escapist quality. The timing of the song was fitting, especially for the gang in an altered state.

High Island lay at what seemed like the end of the world. The cars in their caravan were the only ones on the deserted beach.

Jenny got out of the Challenger, leaving the seat latched, with Lane and James trapped in the back.

"Hey, let me out!" Lane yelled, impatient to be freed. He rattled Kyle's seat with emphasis.

Waking from a dream, James stretched and looked on fondly as Lane shook the seat.

"Hold your horses!" As if in slow motion, Kyle set the parking brake, took his time to pull the seat up, and said, "Here you go."

"Sorry, I was feeling claustrophobic." Lane walked out onto the sand, and his right leg gave way with a tingling sensation.

"What's wrong with you?" James watched Lane stumble around. "You can't be that stoned."

"No, you doofus, my leg's asleep," Lane said, trying to rub it out.

"Who are you calling a doofus?" James chased Lane, who limped around in a circle.

"You!" Lane yelled.

James wrestled him down to the sand.

"Wait!" Lane struggled underneath.

James pinned him and demanded, "Say, uncle."

Lane tried to get out of the stronghold. "Cut it out!"

"Not until you submit," James said smugly, pressing his body against him.

Lane gave in and said, "Uncle," though he didn't mind the closeness.

James slowly rose, leaving Lane uncomfortable for a few seconds more.

"Let me up," Lane said, fighting a slight claustrophobia.

James put out a hand, teeth showing in triumph. "I win."

Lane took James's hand, allowing him to lift his body until he was on his feet. James halfheartedly punched him in the shoulder, making him flinch.

"You may be stronger than me, but you're still a doofus," Lane said, rubbing his shoulder.

"I'm not stupid, man." James walked off.

Lane was confused and looked around the scene. Troy and Don touched up the wax on their surfboards, paying no mind to Tony's rambling. The waves did not seem big enough to surf, but he knew they would try. Kyle and Jenny were having a beer with Riley and Conner near the Jeep truck. The girls made a setup with towels so they could all lay out and catch some rays. Angie slathered lotion on Melissa's tanned back, moving it around the thin strings that tied the green bikini top on.

Lane looked to the sea and saw James brooding. Lane grabbed a couple of beers from the ice chest inside the open car trunk and walked over. "Hey, I brought you a beer."

"Thanks, man." James took a beer and popped it open. Watching the flow of the small surf, he said, "We've got to introduce ourselves to those chicks."

Lane looked across the sand, remembering Dawn and Iris but not knowing the other two. He made a twisted face and said, "Not her."

"No, not her, buddy," James said, brightening, "but we have to be social."

"That's cool," Lane said, resigning himself to the protocol.

The girls in the bikinis reminded him of the *Sports Illustrated* Swimsuit Issue he saw at the gas station. Sara, crouching with her frizzy hair, just needed the caption Don't Just Sit There above her to be a complete cover model.

James led the way, walking a little taller. In a slightly deeper voice, he said, "Hey, how are y'all doing?"

Mid-conversation, the girls stopped and looked up at him like he was a wild animal that had crept up on them. Iris and the tanned girl smiled, but the buxom girl beamed.

Dawn stood up taller than James. "We're doing just fine." She sized them up and asked, "You came with Kyle and Jenny, right?"

"Yeah, Kyle's my roommate. I'm Lane, and this is James." Lane offered his hand, feeling a little out of place.

Dawn shook it with a slight touch. "Dawn. It's a pleasure, I'm sure."

"We came in that sweet ride over there." James stepped closer, pointing at the Challenger, which was shining super-blue in the sun.

"Kyle has a tough car. What do you drive?" Dawn shot him down.

James did not miss a beat. "I have a bike, a BSA Lightning, and it's fast."

With a finger to her pouty lips, Dawn asked, "How come you didn't bring it?"

"Because I rode with them." James kept the moment moving. "Who are the lovely ladies?"

Dawn gave off a flash of distrust, but she turned and introduced her friends. "This is my best friend, Iris."

Iris waved and winked at Lane, and his smile twitched on and off. *I hope this doesn't become one of those situations.*

"And this is Sara." Dawn motioned to the bronze model on her stomach, wiggling her crossed feet to a private chorus in her head. "And Rose, say hello to James."

The big girl jiggled, barely containing her blush as she blurted out, "Hi James."

"Hi." James lost her eye. "So, Sara, do you have a boyfriend?"

Lane rolled his eyes and noticed Iris watching him.

"Maybe." Sara rose up on her elbows, coy. "Why do you want to know?"

"You're too beautiful to be alone, that's all." James squatted down while flirting. His delivery of the line sounded off to Lane.

Dawn changed for the serious. "You two should go."

Lane swallowed and said, "Okay," not liking the new vibe.

"Aw, come on." James shrugged. "I was just warming up to Sara, and I think Iris might like you."

"Maybe we should go," Lane said, rocking in place as his discomfort rose.

James ignored him, continuing to flirt with Sara. "Do you want to go swimming with me?"

"I... I...I can't swim." Sara confessed.

"Really?" James caressed her arm, and the touch sent her a shock.

Lane saw Iris still checking him out and said, "We can come back later."

James threw Lane a look, returned his gaze to Sara, and said, "Well, you know where I'll be if you need a lesson."

"Sure thing." Sara giggled again.

Dawn shooed them away, motioning her head over her shoulder to the jocks. "Sorry, boys. These girls have dates. Sara is with Conner, and Iris is out of the question. And I am—"

"Dawn, who the hell is messing around with you?" A deep, annoyed voice boomed out over the surf.

"With Riley." Lane finished Dawn's sentence.

Riley stormed up, ready to fight. "What do you think you're doing, joker?"

"Hey, man, I was talking to these chicks." James met Riley's cold gaze.

"And they were just leaving," Dawn interjected.

"It's cool, Riley. We're just here to party. We don't want any trouble," Lane said, playing diplomat. He watched the gang gather around and noticed Kyle pulling away from Jenny in the background.

"Anyway, they're not all yours. Are they?" James asked with a dopey smile. He did not see the fist until it was too late.

Riley swung, aiming for James's right eye a second time. A wildly swinging arm blocked his punch, so he aimed lower, jabbing James multiple times in the torso.

Dropping his beer, Lane punched Riley in the neck, receiving a hit in the stomach for his effort. He doubled over, coughing, and watched his foamy beer soak into the sand as he tried to catch his breath.

Riley grabbed his neck, choking. James used the moment to crawl backward. Tony shambled in and knocked Sara onto her rear. A commotion reared up as the mob mentality took over.

In a flash, Conner beat Tony down. Between kicks, he yelled, "Goddamn hippie, try some of this free love!"

Even Sara loomed over Tony, kicking at him with her sandaled foot while yelling, "You dirty bastard!"

"Get off me, you crazy bitch!" Tony tried grabbing Sara's foot to keep her from hitting him again.

Dawn and Iris pulled Sara away as Rose cackled wildly.

"You all right, babe?" Conner consoled Sara, who watched Tony like he was a bug crawling away in the dirt.

Lane, breathing steadily again, dove forward, grabbing a hold of James, who had lunged from the sand to throw a few punches. Riley fought back viciously, out for blood, until a strong arm separated them.

"Enough!" Filled with rage, Kyle glared at the gang.

Riley tried to go at James again, but Kyle manhandled him.

Kyle got in Riley's face and said, "Enough, or I will end you! Do you understand?"

"Hey, they were messing with Dawn," Riley spat, rage in his eyes.

Kyle looked from James to Lane and said, "They obviously didn't know she was your girl, but they do now."

James felt his face and spat, "Stupid jocks are all the same."

"We weren't doing anything, really," Lane pleaded with Kyle.

"Look, Lane is my roommate, and James is his friend. Let's just try to freaking get along," Kyle said and disengaged from Riley, making sure his intent was there.

"Your roommate punched me in the neck," Riley said, putting it out there.

"He did?" Kyle looked at Lane, then nodded in appreciation. Looking back, he said, "Are you worried about that, Riley?"

"No, he just got lucky, and it pisses me off," Riley said.

"Hey, look at them. Do you think they have a shot with your girl?" Kyle dared James or Lane to question it.

"Nah, you're right." Riley cooled out. "Let's drink."

Lane moved James away while the gang's attention moved to Tony, who was yelling.

"Why the hell didn't you help me, Don?" Tony got halfway up, blood running out of the side of his mouth.

Don felt out of place and looked back at Melissa and Angie, who were far away from the fight scene, then at Troy, who was jogging up.

"Don!" Tony yelled.

Searching for a reason, Don found none and said, "It happened so fast." He reached down and grabbed Tony's hand.

"Well, that's fucked up. If it's going to be like this, then I should let you deal with those people from now on," Tony said.

"I don't know what got into me." Don glanced at the ocean.

"Who knows what they would do to you?" Tony clenched his fist.

"I'm really sorry, man." Don shook his head and wished Tony was not there.

"Hey, Kyle!" Tony yelled.

Kyle took in the crowd. "Keep me out of this!"

Don turned his head to the side, then back to Tony. "I promise I'll make it up to you, because this is truly uncool."

Edging farther away with James, a step at a time, Lane said, "One bad scene too many, man."

"I could've taken Riley." James fumed as Lane guided him away.

"You are a fighter, James." Lane put an arm around him in a brotherly way and then pulled it back.

"And you had my back." James moved his jaw around.

"I told you I would," Lane said, lifting his shirt to see if there was a bruise on his stomach. He only saw a round, red mark. James rubbed a finger across it, and Lane flinched.

"Do I look messed up?" James stopped mid-walk to let Lane see his face.

"You'll probably get a black eye, but you look tough," Lane said.

"I do?" James smiled. "Well, alright."

"Yeah, you look good," Lane said.

James noticed Troy and Don, who were carrying their surfboards into the water. "Let's change and go swimming and have a beer."

"Two or three sounds more like it." Lane brightened.

The high-pitched whirring sound of a Volkswagen engine resounded as Ted and Sally drove up, parking next to Troy's Chevy truck. The bug's exhaust gave a sad blowback before it came to a stuttering, stall-like end.

Lane and James shrugged it off and kept their distance, staying outside the gang, which seemed intent on organizing a fire pit of epic proportions.

Lane opened the Challenger's trunk, reached into the chest, and grabbed four beers. "Here you go."

"Why so many?" James asked. A sly look shone out of his unswollen eye.

"We bought them. Why shouldn't we drink them?" Lane grabbed two more cold ones. "Hell, take another."

"I knew there was some reason I liked you." James struggled with carrying three beers, which did not work out well.

Lane saw the situation and said, "Let's chug one to make room."

"Alright, this is just what I need." James set two beers on the bumper, and they perspired, dripping moisture on the metal.

Lane lifted his can, watching James mimic him. He poked the can with a key, puncturing its side. James used a different key and punctured his can with a slosh sound.

"Ready," they said at the same time. Fingers itched on the tabs and lips pressed to the puncture holes. "Set." Their fingernails dug under the tabs. "Go." They pulled the rings and gulped as fast as they could. Beer flowed down their throats like a shotgun blast of liquid and foam. Out of breath, they crumpled the cans together, feeling the buzz.

James looked at the key he used on his can, realizing it was the handcuff key they'd found earlier. "Aw, man, I can't believe I used that."

"You took it," Lane said, staring at its glistening metal edges.

James rotated the key between his fingers. "Do you think they arrested that kid?"

"Nah, I don't think the pigs drop keys like that." He thought of the pollen-covered El Camino with the school books and pack inside. *That kid, Jamie, just got high and left his car at Long John's. What else could it be?* Lane grinned with a wicked thought. "Maybe he's just a freak."

"If you ask me, the whole damn neighborhood is freaky." James picked up a beer from the bumper and popped the top.

Lane opened his own can and looked the motley crew over. Kyle and Riley palled around like buds, Conner cooled off with Sara, and Jenny and Melissa seemed to have made waves with the girls, especially Dawn and Iris. Rose and Sally sat on the sidelines with Ted as Troy and Don swam out on their boards. Tony watched, sitting by himself in a state of exile.

James took in the sights and came to a conclusion. "Fuck all of them. I mean, look at them. They are a bunch of jerks. Hell, I'd rather be an outsider than deal with that scene."

"I am an outsider, James. I don't care about any of them except for Kyle," Lane said. He looked away to watch the shimmer from the heat as it rose off the sand, creating a slight blur in his vision.

"I guess he's cool, but it all just pisses me off." James breathed out, looking at the ocean. "Screw it. Let's change and go swimming, man."

"Cool, I haven't been in the water in ages." Lane lost the melancholy and smiled.

"I thought you came to the beach a lot." James tilted his head.

"Nobody without a board ever wanted to go in the water." Lane twisted his lip.

"Let's do it then." James opened the door to the Challenger. A blue glare greeted him for a second as the sun gleamed off the super-blue paint job.

"Throw me my stuff." Lane held out his hand.

James tossed the towel bundle and then picked up his bundle from the floorboard. "I guess we can change in those dunes over there."

Lane followed James's extended finger to the high dunes in a direction away from the crowd and muttered, "Alright, I'm game."

They walked a few feet, tossing back two more crushed cans, and were popping the last two when Kyle's voice called out, "Hey, help us gather some wood for a bonfire!"

Lane yelled back, "In a bit, we're going swimming!"

"Yeah, I think you have enough muscle to handle it, man!" James yelled.

Lane laughed when there was no reply. He said in a lower voice, "I don't want to get your back again."

"Yeah, that's right." James beamed. "You got my back."

Lane felt weird about the compliment, yet he smiled back.

"Screw them!" James turned and flipped off the crowd, even though no one was paying attention.

"Damn right, screw them!" Lane took a big gulp of Lone Star. "Here's to being an outsider!" He raised his beer.

"Outsiders!" James completed the toast with foam running down his chin.

Lane liked the idea a lot. Outsiders had a ring to it, and it felt right.

EIGHTEEN

Leaving the sightline of the jocks, chicks, and outcasts behind, Lane and James entered the dunes. The trek felt like walking on another planet. There was only some life in the form of wild grass—barely able to survive the shifting and constantly blowing sands—that made up the otherworldly landscape of the coastline.

Lane unrolled his towel, looked at the small gym shorts he brought, and saw a similar pair in James's hands. He pulled off his shirt, feeling very aware of his body compared to James's more built, bare chest.

"I've really got to get some trunks one day," Lane said.

James pulled down his jeans and fumbled with the shorts. "Me too," he said with a sigh.

Lane took off his boots, one at a time, then jeans, but he could not help but look at James, naked and swinging free. His gaze did not go unnoticed. Feeling kind of drafty, he slid up his shorts. James took his time putting his on.

"I hate these shorts." Lane looked away at the dunes. "They're too small."

"That they are." James had a strange vibe, his voice trembling just a little. "Are you ready?"

"Yeah, let's throw this stuff by the car on the way." Lane looked James in the eye again, and it felt okay. All the closeness and contact felt more than brotherly in their eyes. The attraction was there, but neither knew how to put words to it.

"Here," James said, handing Lane a blue pill. "I told you I was saving extra for us."

"Cool. I um..." Lane hesitated.

"Just go with it, man." James put the pill on his tongue and swallowed.

Lane followed down the rabbit hole. "This is righteous."

James got close and smiled. "It is, Lane. It definitely is."

Lane felt the warmth of James's body, the feel of his breath, and the sudden loss when he backed away.

Taking a few more steps, James watched Lane's indecisiveness. "Are we going swimming or what?"

Lane cracked a grin, stepped up, and shoved off. "Race you!"

"Dammit, Lane," James said, pushing himself to keep up. "Hang on!"

Lane, lithe and fast, took the lead. Near the Challenger, he tossed his clothes and mostly empty beer by the car's wheel well. Catching up, James tossed his clothes, too.

A catcall almost threw Lane off balance, but James pushed him onward. He glanced back and saw that it was Iris talking about him to the beach bunnies.

"I told you that girl wants you," James said, panting as he edged closer.

"I beat you!" Lane gloated as he splashed into the salty green water. "I beat you!"

James splashed in at nearly the same time, out of breath. "Just by a hair, that's all!"

They waded deeper, feeling the pull of the tide. Breaking the waves, they went beyond the crashing to the smoother bulge and pull of the sea, where feet did not touch bottom and the strange sensation of living things touched a foot or leg here and there.

The sun blazed down from the side, still searing in the Texas heat. Farther in the ocean and a way to their left, Troy and Don were making the best of the surf. The rest of the gang looked small and isolated, with the growing pile of driftwood and brush gaining some substance as they added to it on shore.

A fin appeared briefly out in the distance, then went underwater.

"You see that?" Lane nudged James.

"See what?" James saw only the rolling water in the tranquility.

"It was a shark, man." Lane pointed. "Right over there."

"Well, I guess we're goners." James shrugged.

"We should go back in." Lane arched his body, preparing to swim.

"Hang on a minute." James grabbed his shoulder while they both treaded water to stay in place.

"What's up?" Lane calmed down as he stared at James, floating in the uneasiness of the moving environment.

"It's probably just a dolphin," James said, not letting go. He pulled Lane in closer, and their kicking legs brushed under the surface.

"So?" Treading water, Lane saw the quizzical look in James's eyes.

James looked around, then gazed at Lane full-on and unafraid. "I saw you checking me out back there."

Lane's heart nearly stopped in his chest. "What? I wasn't checking—"

"Sure, you were. Back in the dunes when we were changing," James said.

"Uh, okay." Lane wanted to look away, but he was in James's grip.

"It's cool." James swallowed and intently stared at Lane. The tide drew their bodies together in the ocean's grip. Out of sight of the others, they were alone. "I mean, do you think I have a hot body?"

Lane felt his heart beat faster. "You do."

James let his hand slide down to Lane's arm. "You're hot too."

"Hey, man, I'm not like those freaks." Lane tensed.

"I know, Lane. You're different." James looked around, then focused. "You're like me."

Lane was slack-jawed. "What the hell? You were trying to pick up Sara. We even got into a fight."

Holding tight to Lane's arm with one hand, James said, "And you went to the drive-in with Tammy last night. Neither of us was interested in fooling around with those girls."

"I don't know what to say," Lane said, spitting out seawater.

"You got it. You can't say anything to anyone," James said.

"Why would I?" Lane felt his pulse racing.

"You must always be tough and fit in," James said, breathing hard. "It's the way of the world. Except in private. Like this." He felt his way down Lane's chest.

"I haven't been—" Lane's words faded into the surf.

"I haven't done much, but I know what I like." James moved closer and reached out with his other hand into Lane's shorts.

Lane's eyes never left James's as his inhibitions dropped, and they explored each other's bodies underwater. His heart beat fast while the surf crashed around them, not unlike a dream or a fantasy. His mouth parted, and he felt lost in James's blue eyes—much bluer than the sky above. He had never touched a guy before, not like this, and it was happening.

A scream rang out, and both of their hands darted away from contact with their flesh.

Lane turned and saw a commotion near the shore. The tide pushed James's body into Lane's. They both pulled away in fear of being caught, despite the spark in their eyes. They'd found each other, and there was no turning back.

"Wow, that freaked me out!" Lane got a mouthful of water.

James exuded sex, shook it off, and said, "Maybe you were right about the shark."

"Look how far we drifted." Lane pointed out the distance from their original spot on the beach.

"The current must've been slowly taking us." James paddled closer and said, "That was hot."

Lane looked at him sideways and smiled. "Yeah, it was."

Together, they floated in the sea, basking in the electric chemistry of attraction.

Lane looked back at the gang surrounding someone on the shore and reluctantly said, "We should get back."

"Alright." James judged the distance. "Race you!" James took off in a splash.

Lane forced his hand over hand, trying to keep up the pace. He was no match, as James was faster in water than on land.

Standing up, a wave crashed into James's back. "I won!"

Lane stood and stumbled into James, who pushed him back. He was about to say something when another, louder scream rang out.

"Come on!" James led the way.

Lane jogged behind him and checked his shorts. He saw James was in the same predicament and hoped it was not obvious enough for anyone to notice before things returned to normal.

In the shallows, Don was lying on the edge of the tidal surf, with Troy and Kyle leaning down and checking out a large series of red welts on his left leg.

The surfboards bobbed on the shore as the water tried to tug them free of the wet sand. A few feet back, the girls whispered amongst themselves while puffing on a joint. Riley, Conner, and Ted were more intent on making snickering jokes than helping Don, who moaned in pain again.

"Quit yapping like a little bitch and let me see your leg." Kyle took control of the situation.

"Goddamn jellyfish stung me!" Don yelled in anguish. He turned his leg so the gang could see.

"It sure seems that way." Troy grimaced.

Kyle examined the wounds. "Yeah, it looks like it got you good."

The movement caused Don to wince. "Great. Well, do something, man." He shook as the water lapped at his legs.

"Well," Kyle said, standing up, "there's only one thing to do."

Troy stood up and grinned. Stepping back, he said, "I'm gonna take your board in, man."

"Okay, be careful with it," Don said, watching Troy as he backed away with a surfboard under each arm. He saw Kyle standing over him. "What are you going to do?"

"Sorry, man, it's the only thing I can do," Kyle said, looking down.

Lane glanced at James, then back at Kyle, and said, "No way."

James chuckled, then his eyes got big. "Damn."

Kyle whipped it out of his shorts. Lane elbowed James, and they exchanged shocked looks.

In realization, Don pleaded, "No, man! What the hell?"

"Gotta piss on it, man. Everyone knows that. Urine is acidic, and it will stop the poison from the jellyfish sting." Kyle held himself steady, not caring who was staring at his manhood. "Don't move, or I might miss."

Don screamed again in disgust as urine spattered the welts on his leg. The group moaned and laughed, not sure how to react to the bizarre sight.

The stream slacked off, and Kyle backed away. "Now, before you get all mad, tell me, does it feel better?"

"Goddamn it, Kyle!" Don sat up in a crouch. "I can't believe you pissed on me!" Stretching his injured leg out, he sighed and said, "It really feels better."

"See, that's what friends are for." Kyle smirked and reached down, pulling Don up.

"If you ever do that again, I'll kill you." Don shook his head. He saw the girls laughing, even Melissa, who had a sorrowful look in her eyes.

"Well, that was better than TV. Man, this trip is getting weird." James smirked and busted up.

"I know. I can't believe that happened." Lane guffawed. "Don will never live that down."

Seawater lapped their feet as Lane and James watched the gang disperse back to the makeshift beach camp.

NINETEEN

JAMES AND LANE HUNGRILY looked at each other. The sweet aroma of burgers on a grill wafted their way.

"That smells good," James said.

"You know what?" Lane bit his lip. "I'm hungry."

"Let's be social then." James touched his face. "And no fighting, I promise."

"Well, I got your back." Lane smiled, but he was not sure how to hide his feelings when looking into those blue eyes.

"I got yours too, pal." James slapped Lane in the rear.

Lane's lips twitched.

"After we eat, maybe we can go play Frisbee or toss a football or something with our new friends over there," James said, halfway glaring behind his grin at Riley and Conner.

"You're going to be trouble," Lane said, looking James over.

"Damn right."

Lane watched James walk ahead, curious about what he had gotten himself into. *I wonder if I can really trust him.* The wind blew in his hair, and he turned and saw Tony skipping shells into the surf. *I feel the way he looks—so out of place and goddamn vulnerable.*

James turned back and said, "Come on."

Jogging over, Lane stood by his side, amazed at how the beach camp had evolved since their swim. A huge deadfall of driftwood and brush arose from a bonfire pit. Around it, the gang had broken into cliques. Riley and Conner controlled the Old Smokey barbecue pit with Dawn, Sara, and Iris. Ken, Sally, and Rose sat off to one side, discussing the corrupt politics of Nixon and the uselessness of the Vietnam War. Closer to the water, Kyle, Jenny, Troy, and Angie talked about recent rock concerts while Don let Melissa tend to him.

"Let's go eat," James said, taking it all in.

"Okay." Lane walked over to Riley and Conner and smiled. "Can I get one of those burgers?"

"No way!" Conner barked and turned away.

"Hey, we just want some burgers," Lane said, comforted by knowing James was behind him.

Riley glanced at the back of Kyle's head and conceded. "Sure. It's Lane, right?"

Lane nodded.

"You've got a hell of a right hook." Riley rubbed his neck.

"Nah, I just got a lucky shot. You could whip me."

"Maybe so, but you've still got some strength for a skinny guy." Riley took a patty off the grill, put it in a bun, and handed it over.

"Give me one too." James ground his teeth a little.

"Here you go." Riley saw Kyle watching him. "I'm sorry about your eye."

"No worries. It was probably just another lucky shot," James said, shifting from side to side.

"Hey, man, I'm trying to be cool." Riley looked over to make sure nobody else was watching.

"Fair enough. Just don't screw with me," James said, letting it go.

"Hey, it's cool, Riley. Thanks for the burgers." Lane kept the peace. "Come on, James, let's eat."

"See you around." James smiled, steely-eyed, at the jock.

"Peace, man," Riley said as they walked away.

"I'll give him a piece," James mumbled.

"Hey, you stood your ground." Lane felt a sense of pride for his new friend.

"I did, didn't I?" James straightened his back.

"Yeah, like I said, you're a fighter." Lane took a bite of his juicy burger, which tasted like charcoal-grilled heaven.

James whispered in Lane's ear, "I'll wrestle you later."

Lane nearly choked on his food and whispered back, "I hope so."

James took a bite. "Damn, this is good."

Lane chewed his mouthful as they walked up to the gang. "What's going on, guys?"

"Sit over here by me." Jenny patted the ground to her left.

"There are already some beers out for y'all," Kyle said, motioning to some cans stuck and twisted in the sand.

"Thanks, man." James picked up one and passed the other to Lane.

Lane sat Indian style, legs crossed, and surveyed their clique. "How's the leg, Don?"

"I don't want to talk about it," Don mumbled, closing his eyes again while Melissa put the wet corner of a towel on his forehead.

James tried to copy Lane's sitting position, but his legs were not bendy enough to manage it. "How do you do that?"

"It's easy." Lane showed how by folding his legs again.

"Hell, I need to run again. I quit when the coach cut me," James said.

"You were on the track team?" Troy looked at James in wonder.

"Did you think I was a born stoner?" James feigned shock.

"You just don't seem like the type." Angie toked on a freshly lit joint.

"I'm full of surprises, I guess." James winked at Lane.

"Speaking of surprises, stay away from those chicks." Kyle took a hit.

"It's cool. In fact, we just made peace with Riley." Lane made his point and chomped on some more of his burger.

"Yeah, it's cool. And I'm sorry for causing a scene," James said, taking on Kyle's level gaze.

"That's all right." Kyle passed the joint to James. "You seem like a cool cat."

"Hey, look," Jenny said, showing off her new jewelry. "I made a tab ring necklace."

"That's mighty nice," Lane raised an eyebrow to Kyle's chagrin.

"By the end of the night, everyone could have one." James poked fun.

"I'll have to make some more." Jenny giggled in a cloud of smoke.

Troy, biting into his own burger and chewing with his mouth open, asked, "What's with the burnout? Tony, I mean."

Lane followed Troy's judgment to the sea. "Tony has had some rough times, that's all."

"We've all had rough times growing up, but we try." Troy looked at Angie for support. "Ain't that right, babe?"

"He's disgusting." Angie turned away. "He's trash."

"Well, he used to be my friend." James sighed. "But he changed."

"Leave him alone, and he'll find his way." Kyle dismissed the sight.

"You know, I treat him badly all the time, but he's living on the streets." Lane stood up and stretched. "I'm going to talk to him."

"Why?" Angie asked with disdain.

"Because Tony's stuck here with us." Lane looked to James for reassurance, but James looked away.

"That's really sweet, Lane." Melissa broke the tone and eyed the other guys one by one. "You guys could learn something from him."

Don purposely groaned, grabbing her attention.

"It's going to be all right, Donnie Bear," Melissa cooed.

Troy whispered something to Kyle, and they laughed.

"I'll be right back." Lane stepped off, feeling alone again.

Tony was in silhouette on the shore, standing and watching the light change over the restless water as the sun slowly descended. Lane approached with caution, feeling like he was invading Tony's space. A wave crashed, and he considered turning back.

Tony stopped mid-throw of a shell, palming it to his side. "Why don't you go back over there with your friends, Lane?"

"Only if you come with me," Lane said.

"You never want to hang out back home, man," Tony said, squinting to lessen the blinding sun.

"That's because you're pretty damn needy." Lane felt light-headed.

"I ain't got a place to go half the time." Tony looked away at a boat far out on the horizon.

"You manage," Lane said, stepping away a little.

Tony nodded, then widened his eyes in shock.

"What's doing, Tony?" James pulled out the empty bag of the blue pills, and his voice shook with an edge to it. "Did you know those were bunk?"

Surprised, Tony held out his hand. "Let me see." He checked the residue in the bag with a finger.

James said, "Lane, are you feeling anything yet?"

Lane thought about his high. "Not really. I'm a little stoned, but I don't feel any different from how I usually do."

"Give me my money back." James shook his head.

"Wait a minute, man. Those were lighter, weren't they? I must've given you the wrong ones." Tony reached into his jeans, brought out a bag of darker blue pills, and traded for the loss.

James rolled the six around in his hand, thinking it over. "These better be real."

"These are my personal stash, man. So, it's cool." Tony fidgeted, avoiding their eyes.

"Here you go, Lane, two for you and two for me." James put two pills on his tongue and swallowed them.

Lane looked at James, followed his action, and said, "Vitamins are delicious."

"We'll see." James glared at Tony. "We'll see."

"Trust me, y'all are in for a trip." Tony put his stash down in his pants. "Damn, I can't believe y'all took two."

"Hey, boss, where's mine?" Kyle swaggered in.

Brushing the hair out of his face, Tony turned on a smile. "Here, these two are for you and your chick. Don't give her a whole pill if you want a fun night," he warned.

"Right on. I don't want her to just lie there." Kyle looked at him and bit one in half as he swaggered back to the fire.

"Do you think we messed up taking two?" Lane felt a little nervous at the prospect.

"Nah, it's cool." James looked at the sinking sun. "It's going to be beautiful, man."

"Cool. Just don't let me be foolish." Lane watched the sun turn orange.

"No worries." James put an arm around Lane. "We're pals now."

"Pals, I can dig it." Lane moved his arm around James, knowing 'pals' meant something else now. *Maybe we can hit the road on his bike.*

Lane felt the darkness all around, but he could hear voices and the surf. The blue pills were pulling at his mind. James sat on a log next to him, his arm grazing his back, as the fire roared to life with the flick of Riley's lighter and some siphoned gasoline from Troy's truck. The heat was intense. The hungry flames crackled and snapped into the driftwood, rushing through the tinder and brush.

The fire lit up strange faces. Lane felt a hand touch his lower back. The contact brought his attention to James's orange-lit face. He laughed, and he heard an echo of the laughter that haunted him.

Above, the stars seemed so far away, yet the clarity of their pinpoints was amazing. The sky turned into the colors of space, rich in blues and blacks.

Lane rose to a new plateau of being high. His body felt like it was somewhere else in another time and place, and he sensed himself from afar. He looked at James's profile in the inferno's light, feeling a closeness to him. *We could just ride away into a sunset like this one—ride west—until we can ride no more.*

The brush crackled, and flames rushed around it like a living thing that was trying to escape into another world.

"Check out the fire. It rises to lick the night sky with a thousand orange tongues." Lane laughed, trying to convince James of his vision.

"Aw, man, I see them." James was on the same wavelength. "They have forked tongues."

"This reminds me of this dream I had last night," Lane said.

"What was it about?" James watched the sparks drift up.

"It was me and you on a spaceship—no, a space station—wearing spacesuits that kind of looked like gas station coveralls." Lane stumbled over his words. "And like this thing..." Lane motioned. "Skylab fell out of orbit, burning like a comet. Then there was this black hole, and we were floating towards it."

"Me and you, huh?" James muttered.

"Yeah. You told me something in the dream," Lane said.

"What's that?" James wavered.

"You said something was coming." Lane flinched from the crackling fire. "The chaos is here now."

"That's tripped out." James's forehead creased in thought. "You know, I don't even remember most of my dreams."

"I have been lately," Lane said and tuned in to the radio. DJ Crash promised more Pink Floyd from the dash, and he delivered "A Saucerful of Secrets". The heavily tripped-out track strangely reverberated from the car stereos.

"I wish I remembered." James bit his lip. "What else do you see?"

"I see some naked freaks." Lane nodded his head, and Dawn, Iris, and Sara seemed far away, bouncing and swaying with Conner and Riley in a sea of skin.

James looked at the gang around the fire. "Oh wow, it looks like a commune out there."

In the alternating darkness and the flashing light of the fire, Lane noticed Ted making out with Rose and Sally. "This is like a *Lord of the Flies* skin flick."

"I dig it, all tribal and such." James watched the dancers, getting an eyeful. "Hey, where is Kyle?"

Lane turned around, and the sight felt like a melting, slow-motion blur, trying to keep focus. "Whoa!"

"What?" James pulled up his jaw.

Inside the Challenger, a rough hand slid across the fogged-up glass of the back window.

Lane said, "Kyle's in the car, grooving down with Jenny."

James stared at the handprint. "They better not mess up my clothes."

"I've got to go to the dunes and take a piss." Lane stood up. The world whooshed by, and he stumbled.

"Whoa there," James said, trying to catch Lane. He stumbled himself. "Wow, I'm kind of fucked up, too."

"This is beautiful, man." Lane swayed as he looked at the bodies on display.

"Come on, Lane. I've got to piss too." James grabbed Lane's arm, and they weaved away from the fire and the music.

Something was strange about the view of the beach. Under the waxing moon, the light was choppy through the passing clouds. Lane felt that walking with James was difficult, as if the sand were shifting underfoot as they trudged to the dunes. His coordination was off with each ill-placed step, and he let James lead him up and over a sand ridge. The sea breeze picked up a notch, and the sounds of the beach party drifted away, but the urge to pee overrode the eeriness.

Lane stopped, pulled the front of his shorts down, and waited a long moment before relief hit with a stream. He heard an accompanying sound and saw James at his side, struggling not to pee on their feet.

"Hey, man, watch it." Lane moved his leg out of the way.

"Don't worry. It'll keep it from burning." James tittered.

They crossed streams, leaving a weird, wet pattern in the sand. A thud of metal sounded out of the night.

Lane stopped urinating and listened. "Did you hear that?" he asked in a whisper.

"I don't. No, wait—" James leaned back his head, and his own stream tapered out. "There's something out there."

Lane pulled his shorts up, and his eyes locked on James. He heard a sloshing noise and said, "Get down."

James tucked himself away and dove, hiding in the dunes with Lane.

The sloshing noise sounded in tandem, one mimicking the other, as Lane concentrated on movement in the dark. In his altered state, his vision faltered. *Dammit, I've got to get my snap.*

James's heart was beating fast as another slosh echoed out, and he whispered, "I think there's a car out there."

Lane breathed out and focused. He made out the contours of a familiar dark-red GTX with the trunk open in the shifting moonlight. A few feet away from the car, two shadowy figures were digging a deep hole.

"No way," Lane whispered. "That's the car, man. That's the GTX I've been seeing everywhere!"

"What are they doing?" James struggled to see more clearly.

"It can't be good. We've got to go." Lane turned and slipped, breaking a small cascade of loose sand.

The slide covered James's feet, and he disappeared over the side.

Lane was alone, and he froze as the figures stopped digging and looked in his direction. The wind blew sand in his eyes, but he dared not wipe them. He heard rustling and crawled backwards, uncertain if what he was seeing was real or not. One shadow set down a shovel and slowly approached.

The world in his view turned and refocused, then a strong hand grabbed Lane's face. Panic set in, and he struggled until he saw the blue eyes in the moonlight.

James inhaled and whispered, "Stay low and let's go."

Lane nodded in acquiescence. They stealthily moved along the side of the dune and stood up in a patch of tall pampas grass.

Panting, James swatted at the grass blades and fluffy stalks like it was a hallucination.

Lane felt queasy and said, "I think I'm going to be sick," and he vomited into the weeds, full force.

"Come on, Lane, stay with me." James concentrated. He placed Lane's limp arm over his shoulder and half-walked, half-carried him back onto the beach.

Lane turned and saw a figure in the dunes—where they just were—staring from the shadows. "Oh man, that was close."

"Yeah, that was weird. Did they see us?" James picked up the pace with Lane, and Kyle suddenly appeared at their side, startling him.

"Is he all right?" Kyle took on some of the burden of Lane's dead weight.

"He just threw up, that's all." James snuck a look over his shoulder and saw no one in the dunes.

"Yeah, there were some people digging back there," Lane spat, drooling a little.

"I don't want him getting sick in my car," Kyle warned.

"Leave him with me by the fire." James beckoned to the log they had left earlier.

The gang paid them no notice, oblivious and high, as they approached.

"Alright, just make sure he's okay before we take off later on." Kyle looked eagerly back at the Challenger.

"Yeah, I got it." James nodded to the car. "Get back to Jenny."

"Am I dying?" Lane looked up to see James's face haloed by the flames.

"No. You are just wasted... Like me." A strange grin spread across James's face as he felt the buzz catch up to him.

"I like you," Lane said as the fire changed into smoke and billowed across the night.

"Right on." James let Lane lie across his lap.

"Hey, James—" Lane's words drifted off as the smoke faded away.

PART FOUR

NIGHT SURF

TWENTY

A SEA BREEZE BLEW through the dunes as a rough hand parted the pampas grass blades. Eyes full of malice stared at the wild teens partying around the bright bonfire burning on the remote beach. The shadowy figure had watched the two boys stumble and weave as they left the dunes, close enough to see the forbidden. In the glare of the dim light, he thought it was Lane.

How poetic, he thought, *that he should see me. Because I see him.*

He saw another teen help him make it to where they were on the log, Lane—he was sure of it now—lying on the other's lap in the orange glow.

Another shadow leaned down beside him and whispered, "That one looks familiar. His name is James."

A third shadow called out with a short bark in the wind. The other two shadows left the view of the fire and returned to dig in silence. The crashing surf buried the soft music from the car radios on the other side of the dunes. The tide was coming in under intermittent moonlight.

Two figures hoisted a plastic-wrapped body out of the trunk of the red GTX and tossed it into the pit. One ripped open a heavy bag, and white powder flurried down. Hands worked quickly in succession, shoveling sand over the plastic and burying it all.

The clouds covered the moon, and the car rumbled to life, leaving the site behind in the darkness.

"I'm coming for you, Lane," he whispered into the wind. "My special boy."

ONE OF THE THREE burial sites of the killers—the others were a wooded area near Lake Sam Rayburn and a boat storage shed in southwest Houston—was a lonely stretch of beach near High Island on the Gulf Coast.

Days after the story broke on August 8th, 1973, law enforcement excavated six bodies from lime-covered graves near the dunes. The police called off the search of all sites within a week of discovering the 27th body, leaving some of the missing boys unaccounted for and their reasons for calling it off unknown.

Hurricane Ike, in 2008, eroded the coast-line and submerged the burial site below sea level. The lost boys left behind are still down there.

Acknowledgments

It took a ton of research and a funeral to create *Summer 1973*, and I could not have done it without the people I met along the way.

I would like to thank my partner, Bo, for giving me the space to write and supporting my craft over the years. He has also championed this story in its many iterations, keeping me from taking the easy way out.

My sincere appreciation goes to David-Jack Fletcher for surprising me with a New Year's Eve email stating interest in the manuscript two years after passing on it. He has been a solid editor and has helped me shape and give balance to the material.

The seed of the story was planted when Larry Crawford gave me and a friend an after-hours showing of an exhibit of serial killer art at the Hyde Park Gallery in 1997. Elmer Wayne Henley's still-life of surreal sunflowers and his seascape with green grass growing in the dunes disturbed me as much as a victim's family member protesting by burning a painting on the street at the art opening. I had no idea I would be writing about the true crime years later.

In 2008, the case had come back in the news with new DNA evidence identifying remains and correcting prior mistakes. Crawford approached me about writing a story about the art, so I decided to learn about the murders.

There is nothing as creepy as hanging out in the Reading Room of the haunted Julia Ideson Building of the Houston Public Library. At that time, there were only two out-of-print books about the murders, both published in 1974. I found a used copy of *The Man With the Candy* by Jack Olsen, but I had to read *Mass Murder in Houston* by John K. Gurwell in the old room. Under the dim lighting, it was easy to believe ghosts walked the aisles.

Newspapers and video media were difficult to find when I started this project. I explored the library's microfiche archives of *The Houston Post* and *Chronicle*, finding stories from August 8th, 1973, when the crimes became known through the discovery of the bodies and the subsequent trials (1974–1979) of Henley and Brooks, the teenage accomplices. The 1981 mondo documentary, *The Killing of America*, had a segment about the murders, and the 2000 film *Collectors* focused on serial killer art, showing the images I saw in person at the gallery.

In researching the crimes, I had the invaluable assistance of David Babb, who worked for the Harris County Coroner and KPFT 90.1 Pacifica Radio. He helped me find all the existing true crime locations from the Heights to the boat shed and introduced me to gay activist Ray Hill. Ray had civic connections and knew a lot about the city's history even though he was in prison for jewelry theft when the story of the murders broke. I talked to him a bit about the Heights neighborhood and gay life of the time, and he even had me sit in on a live broadcast of his call-in radio program, *The Prison Show*, an outreach program for inmates and their families.

Sharron Derrick, the forensic anthropologist, could not identify one victim, ML73-3356, John Doe 1973, aka Swimsuit Boy. Through Ray Hill, I met her when I attended the boy's funeral in November 2009 at a pauper's field where they bury criminals and unidentified persons. The reconstructed photo of him at the graveside with his statistics, clothes, manner of death, and where they found him in the boat shed haunted me. I decided then and there that the story was going to be different, inspired by this lost boy.

When I was writing the first draft, I did some promotional gigs with Chris Binum, an actor who was filming *In a Madman's World*, Josh Vargas's now lost film. He played the teenage killer, Henley, and tried to get me an extra part, but I was moving to Chicago at the time. The incomplete film is notable for Marilyn Burns, star of *The Texas Chain Saw Massacre*, in her final role as Mrs. Hill, a victim's mother. So many weird connections come into play when you work on a project.

I appreciate the feedback I received from Preston Fassel when he was story editor for Cinestate, which owned *Fangoria* magazine and was producing movies and books. He encouraged me to continue to work on the manuscript by writing to me about how it was a commendable goal to take on a gay coming-of-age story set in 1973 and the importance of humanizing the victims who lost their lives. It was the best rejection I ever got from a submission.

I hope the *Summer 1973* series brings attention to the lost boys who are still missing, the ones who never ran away and ended up in a shallow grave.

About the Author

Dean Cade is a Gen X writer who survived the chaos of running wild on the streets in his formative years. Now he uses those experiences—the highs, lows, and the redemptions—to write memoir and genre fiction. A lifelong film and horror fan, he spends his free time lifting weights. Dean lives in Texas with his partner, Bo, and their Siberian Husky, Max. deancade.com.

Summer 1973 is his debut, the first in a trilogy, and a unique combination of true crime and horror.